Echoes of the Past

By

Anita Osborn

To Nancy
with my best
Wishes!
Anita

* * *

Printed in Victoria, Canada

National Library of Canada Cataloguing in Publication Data

A cataloguing record for this book that includes the U.S. Library of Congress Classification number, the Library of Congress Call number and the Dewey Decimal cataloguing code is available from the National Library of Canada. The complete cataloguing record can be obtained from the National Library's online database at: www.nlc-bnc.ca/amicus/index-e.html

ISBN 1-4120-1578-2

TRAFFORD

This book was published *on-demand* in cooperation with Trafford Publishing.
On-demand publishing is a unique process and service of making a book available for retail sale to the public taking advantage of on-demand manufacturing and Internet marketing. **On-demand publishing** includes promotions, retail sales, manufacturing, order fulfilment, accounting and collecting royalties on behalf of the author.

Suite 6E, 2333 Government St., Victoria, B.C. V8T 4P4, CANADA
Phone 250-383-6864 Toll-free 1-888-232-4444 (Canada & US)
Fax 250-383-6804 E-mail sales@trafford.com
Web site www.trafford.com TRAFFORD PUBLISHING IS A DIVISION OF TRAFFORD HOLDINGS LTD.
Trafford Catalogue #03-1955 www.trafford.com/robots/03-1955.html

10 9 8 7 6 5 4 3 2 1

Dedications

To Bill, my husband and best friend.

With thanks and gratitude for your constant support, encouragement and unconditional love.

I love you!

To Steve, Don and Jenny, my children,

I will love you always!

Forward

The purpose for writing my Memoirs is so that my children and grandchildren will know where I came from. I want them to know my life's story in detail, know about the happy events as well as the sad ones and understand that my heritage is part of their own heritage as well. The events in this book might not always be politically or historically correct, but I wrote the events as I remembered them and perceived them.

The hardships, joys and triumphs that I have experienced in my life are a testimony to my belief in God. My fervent wish is that these pages will be encouragement to those who read them and that my favorite Scripture verse will become as real to them as it has become to me.

I can do all things through Christ

who strengthens me - Phil. 4:11

Acknowledgements

I would like to thank my family and my many friends who have encouraged me to write this book.

My special thanks to:

Eva Grohmann, Peggy Ross and Fred Wilhelm, (my sisters and brother) who helped with so many dates, names and details of my story;

Hans Wilhelm (my brother) who translated my father's biography, letters and quotes from the Liebenzell Mission archives;

Phyllis Weichenthal, whose encouragement helped to get this project started, and to Shirley Mead for her conscientious editing expertise. I am grateful to you both;

Debrah Rafel for her help with the cover design and layout;

And finally, to my son, Don, for formatting and layout, and your loving support and patience.

Table of Contents

* * *

1

First Sight of America

It was early in the morning while most passengers on the luxury liner, the S.S. United States, were still in bed when the voice of the ship's Captain was heard on the loudspeakers saying: "Attention, now hear this! THE LADY IS IN SIGHT and can be seen from the upper deck."

My sister Eva and I dressed and hurriedly went to the upper deck to join the many passengers who had heard the message from the Captain. Far in the distance we saw a very small statue. We stayed on deck and watched the ship sail into the harbor of New York where we saw the magnificent Statue of Liberty in all her glory. It was an awesome sight.

"So, this is America," I thought, "where my life will have a new beginning." The date was March 19, 1953.

Forty-three years later in June of 1996 I saw the Statue of Liberty for a second time. A regional choir called The Valley Voices that I sing in was invited to perform at Carnegie Hall, joining 350 singers from around the country. We performed "Brahms Requiem," under the direction of Helmut Rilling, a well-known conductor from Germany. We sang the work in German, which was especially meaningful for me, and being able to coach my fellow-singers in my native language was so enjoyable. The Concert was a wonderful experience and a thrilling and memorable occasion.

Later that evening we took a midnight cruise around the harbor of New York. The lights of the city were fantastic and soon we came upon the wonderful landmark, The Statue of Liberty. She was illuminated and breathtakingly beautiful. Emotions were running high, and there was absolute silence aboard the boat, until one voice started singing "America the Beautiful." The rest of the choir joined in as we sailed by the Statue of Liberty as well as Ellis Island. It was an incredible moment that I will not soon forget. Memories came to mind of the time I saw the Statue for the first time so many years ago.

I felt truly blessed and privileged to be living in this great country.

2
From Germany to China

I was born on March 5, 1932 in Hungkiang, province Hunan, in the Interior of China. I was the third child, born to Karl Max and Anna Elizabetha Giessel Wilhelm. My parents were German missionaries living in China, working for The Liebenzell Mission.

My father was born February 28, 1896 in Zschorlau, Saxony, in the eastern part of Germany. His parents were Oskar and Ida Wilhelm and he was the oldest of ten children. His childhood was a happy one and he was raised in a committed Christian home. At an early age he decided to become a missionary. He allowed nothing to interfere with his desire. He served in World War I, where he was awarded **The Iron Cross First Class** (das Eiserne Kreuz 1. Klasse), one of the highest awards given for bravery.

Following the war he proceeded with his ministerial and Christian education. It took five years of training and preparation in a Mission Seminary in Bad Liebenzell, a beautiful little resort town in southern Germany. In 1923, my father completed his education and was commissioned to China to begin his first term as a missionary.

While visiting his family in eastern Germany, he made the acquaintance of Anna Elisabetha Giessel, who was a young Deaconess working in an orphanage near his hometown. Anna had come from Offenburg, Baden in the western part of Germany.

I do not know much of my Mother's early life. She was the second youngest child in a family of six and grew up not knowing her father. When she was only two years old, her father disappeared and was never heard of again. He went on his customary Sunday morning walk in the wooded park in Offenburg on May 1st of 1897 and no one ever saw him again. The only clue was that his tailor's scissors disappeared along with him. He was a Master Tailor by profession and his scissors were his best tool of the trade. After a thorough search of his whereabouts, it became apparent that it was futile to continue the search of my grandfather, Karl Giessel, and it was assumed that he emigrated to another country. The disappearance for Karl Friedrich Giessel has always been a mystery.

It was a severe shock to his wife Anna Maria Giessel. She was left to raise her children on her own. The youngest child, a son, Richard, was not born yet when his father disappeared. My grandmother's parents, Peter and Maria Cron, were never in favor of their daughter's marriage to my grandfather, but helped her and her children financially after her husband left her. The Crons were a very devout Catholic family, and Karl Giessel, who was from Pommern, a state in northeast Germany, was Protestant. At that time it was unacceptable and a disgrace to marry outside of your family's religion.

I was told that my grandmother Giessel was very good-natured and steadfast, even during her time of struggles. She did some housecleaning and ironing for people with means to make ends meet. It must have been quite humbling for her, but she did what she had to do. Anna Maria's parents were groundskeepers at the Castle of Stolzenfels, near Koblenz. It is a beautiful castle located high on the left bank of the Rhein River, surrounded by very lush and productive vineyards. The Crons, my grandmother's parents, were owners of vineyards in that same area and produced a "Weinbrand," a type of brandy in their own distillery, beginning in 1894. The name of their product was called "Maria Cron" and is available to this day. When the estate of the Crons was settled, my grandmother was awarded very little of the sizeable inheritance. It was said that she received her share from her parents while bringing up her family. Anna Maria Giessel died

August 13, 1938. She was 77 years old. I am very sorry that I was never able to meet her.

Mutti, my mother, must have been raised Protestant, unless she changed from Catholicism to being a Protestant in her later years. She became a deaconess with a sisterhood in Miechowitz in Oberschlesien, a state in Eastern Germany, and dedicated her life to homeless children. She was working in an orphanage called "Friedenshort," which means "Peaceful Sanctuary." It was so appropriately named for an orphanage.

On several occasions young Max Wilhelm came to visit little orphan friends at the orphanage and it was on these visits that he noticed the pretty brunette Anna Giessel and became quite interested in her. However, he never had the opportunity to speak to her in private. Shortly before the departure to his assigned mission field in China, he wrote to Anna asking her to be his life partner.

This was a complete surprise to Anna. She had only considered Max Wilhelm to be a good friend and had not entertained any other thoughts of him beyond that. It took many hours of prayer and much consideration before she made her decision to marry Max Wilhelm and follow him to China. However, Anna had to get special permission from the Sisterhood to take this tremendous step in her life, which was truly a leap of faith.

They were able to spend a short time together before Max left for China on December 4, 1923. His first stop in China was Chinkiang, the location of the Training Home and Language School of the China Inland Mission. The task there was to conquer the "language mountain." In the course of the next two years, young missionary Wilhelm was stationed in Yuanchow and Hungkiang. (Province Hunan) and Sankiang (Province Kweichow.)

* * *

His bride-to-be Anna, whom he had left behind, attended the training school for the sisters for the Liebenzell Mission at Liebenzell for the next two years until she was commissioned on September 13, 1925 and designated for China. She arrived in China and entered language school, where she was soon informed of the sad news that her fiancé, Max Wilhelm, had been captured by bandits and was being held for a huge ransom. Mission policy did not allow for any ransom payments. He spent almost five days in the mountain quarters of the bandits, but was released unharmed by Chinese soldiers.

* * *

In accordance with the requirements of the Mission at that time, the wedding could not take place until the bride had been in the country for two years and had passed her Second Language Exam. After this prolonged period of waiting, the couple was finally married on September 2, 1927 in the little mission chapel in Hungkiang. It was a quiet and simple wedding, attended only by a few fellow missionaries and several Chinese friends. Their honeymoon was spent traveling on a small Chinese boat towards their new Mission-station.

* * *

During the years of 1927-1932 my parents were stationed in Sankiang, Kweichow working hard to fulfill their missionary duties. They worked hard, but were happy and content doing the Lord's work among the Chinese people, whom they had come to love very much. Times were hard and they were often plagued by malaria. Two children were born to them in Sankiang, Eva Maria and Hans Martin.

Shortly after my birth on March 5, 1932, my family began their trip to Germany for their first furlough. Eva Maria was 3 years old, Hans Martin was 1½ years old and I was only 17 days old when the long journey was begun. Mutti (as our mother was called) and I arrived in Germany very sick and were entrusted to my Grandmother Wilhelm's care. I was told later that a good friend in Zschorlau, the hometown of my father, where we lived, called me "Friedhofs Bluemchen" which means "Little Cemetery Flower." I was not expected to live. My Grandmother, whom I called Mother, nurtured me to health and literally spoon-fed me, to become stronger and healthier.

My parents spent the next 2½ years of their furlough traveling all over Germany doing deputation work, speaking and preaching the gospel to promote their mission work, and raising funds for the Liebenzell Mission.

During that time two more children were born to them, Esther Elizabeth and Karl Friedrich.

In March of 1935, the family of six returned for a second time to China. However, I was left behind in the care of my paternal grandparents in Zschorlau, Saxony.

3
My Childhood in Germany

I was three years old when my parents left me behind and I only have one memory of my father. I still remember the room and have a very vivid picture in my mind being there with my father. Evidently I was naughty, or did something that he scolded me for when I said to him: "You can't scold me, you are not my father, you are just my uncle." I got spanked for saying that. But I am sure that in my mind, it was my Grandfather who was my father, not Papa, whom I only saw on occasions. It must have made quite an impact on me because that is the only memory I have of my father, and it is a sad memory.

* * *

Ida and Oskar Wilhelm became my parents. I called them father and mother and loved them dearly. I especially had a very close relationship with my grandfather. He was an extraordinary man. By the time I came to live with my grandparents my grandfather was already retired.

What I remember mostly about my grandfather was that he instilled in me an appreciation of God's wonderful nature as he took me to nearby forests to gather blueberries and wild mushrooms. I loved these outings and learned a lot from Father. He taught me which mushrooms were good to eat and which ones were poisonous.

On the days my grandfather and I gathered mushrooms our meal always consisted of fried mushrooms and fried potatoes. That was one of my favorite meals. The blueberries in our forests grew on low bushes that covered the ground on the outskirts of the forests. The berries were plentiful, very sweet and juicy, and made wonderful blueberry pancakes

Father was small of stature, but had a big heart and to me he was as big as a giant. I really looked up to him and he taught me so much that will stay with me for the rest of my life.

My grandmother was a very strong personality and was the Matriarch of the Wilhelm family. I remember her being ill much of my childhood. My best memory of "Mother" is that I could always tell her everything that was on my mind. She was interested in all of my school activities, outside interests, innermost feelings, girlfriends, and later on my boyfriends.

We lived in a house that had been a beautiful villa at one time, but was converted into several apartments.

My grandparents and I lived in one of the apartments on the second floor of the house, which we called "the Bochman house." It was nice, and we had several spacious rooms. The owner of the house was Frau Bochman. She was a very mean and difficult lady to have as a landlord. My friend Inge, who was also my cousin, and I were always afraid of her and often called her the "Witch". She had that kind of an aura about her. Inge and I often got into trouble with my grandmother for hassling Frau Bochman. We mimicked her, rang her doorbell and went into hiding when she came to answer the door. Heaven forbid if we ran up and down the stairs and made any kind of noise, nor were we ever allowed to play in her big yard that had many fruit trees. She was afraid that we might steal an apple or a pear.

I loved the little brick road that led to our home. It was so quaint and was framed with lilac and snowball bushes.

Our good friends, the Voigt Family, lived close to us. They had a home of their own and his dental office was on the first floor of the house. They had three daughters and a son. I always admired them so as a child. They were several years older than I was, but were very nice and friendly to me. I remember going to the dental office one day and asking Mrs. Voigt if I could get a gold tooth from her dentist husband like I had seen in the mouth of my grandfather. I was so disappointed when I was told that I was too young to have a gold tooth in my mouth.

Living in an apartment never allowed me to have any pets. None of my cousins or close friends had pets either, so I did not feel underprivileged or deprived.

From a very young age I remember being told that my parents were missionaries in China and that I was left behind because I was not healthy enough to make the trip back to China. The whole village of Zschorlau was extremely proud of my father and held him in high esteem. My father was the first man from the village to go to a foreign country to be a missionary. He and my mother both were put on a pedestal and remained there as long as I can remember. I was very proud to be the daughter of missionaries. I never knew the circumstances or the reasons that lay behind the decision to leave me behind in Germany.

* * *

I was later told that my parents had anticipated coming back home to Germany to re-unite with me in five to seven years, but the Second World War broke out, thus preventing them from returning to Germany.

So I grew up in Zschorlau, a very picturesque little village in the heart of the "Erzgebirge" in Sachsen, Germany. When I was six years old, I was enrolled in grade school, along with my cousin Inge Zschiedrich who was my constant mate. We were the same age and the best of friends.

When we returned from our first day of school, Mother was waiting for us. She was leaning out of the open window, as was the custom, and similar to sitting on the front porch waiting for someone to come home. As we approached the house, Inge shouted to her, "Anita can't go back to school. She didn't understand the lesson. She is not smart enough". Mother replied," Why don't you come in and we will talk about it." I was almost convinced by Inge that I did not need to go back to school, because I would not make it anyway.

One of my favorite games to play was hopscotch. Inge and I, with some other friends, played it by the hour and had so much fun doing it. I don't remember having a lot of toys, but I had some little dolls that I liked to play with.

I loved playing the board game "Mensch aergere Dich nicht" (Parcheesi) with father or Inge; often father would let me win so I would not get too discouraged.

My early childhood was happy and I always felt loved by my grandparents. Many aunts, uncles and cousins surrounded me. They were my family.

I always knew that I had another mother and father and sisters and brothers in China, but that was so far away and I knew so little about them. The distance between us was so great and they were in essence unreachable. Now and then I received some pictures from my family in China, which I studied with great interest, wishing I could be part of the family that I did not know.

4
Beginning of World War II

In 1939 the Second World War broke out. I remember how concerned the adults were and how often the discussion centered on the leader of Germany, Adolf Hitler, and what might be happening in the near future.

Several of my uncles and other relatives were drafted into the Military.

There were lots of tears and heartbreak, as they had to leave their families. My Grandmother was sad so much of the time and the laughter I had known earlier was happening less and less.

Our church in Zschorlau was an Evangelical Lutheran church. There was also a Methodist church in our village, as well as the "Gemeinschaft," which was a fundamental branch of the main Lutheran Church, which was the State Church. We went to the Gemeinschaft on Sunday afternoons and most of my family was active in it. However, the Gemeinschaft was only for fellowship meetings and other get-togethers. My grandfather was often invited to preach in neighboring meetings on Sunday evenings and I liked to accompany him so he didn't have to walk the lonely country roads by himself.

Weddings, funerals, confirmations and baptisms were only held in the State Lutheran Church. I loved that church. It was very old and had a beautiful pipe organ. The church was built in 1652. I was baptized and confirmed there.

When I was in grade school I sang in a children's church choir that was called "Kurrende." Mr. Grosser was our "Kantor," (Organist and Music Director) an outstanding musician, and director of our Kurrende. He played the organ with such vigor and enthusiasm. It was a joy to listen to him playing. Many years later, when I met the British Composer, John Rutter, I thought of Mr. Grosser. They resembled each other in many ways.

We all wore black robes with big white collars and sang for special occasions, especially at funerals. The funeral procession was led by the Kurrende and followed by the hearse and the family. The person leading the Kurrende carried a large Golden Cross on a long pole that was very heavy. The funeral procession assembled at the house of the deceased and walked through the village on to the church and the cemetery. The cemetery was located around the church. The gravesites were planted with flowers and groundcover and were beautifully kept and tended to by the families. It was an evening outing to go to the cemetery to water the flowers on the graves. For widows, it was a ritual to visit the graves of their loved one daily.

Our cemetery was relatively small within the confines of a gated area, including the church. Graves were recycled and after a certain amount of years dug up and used again. One morning Inge and I watched as the grave of our Great Grandmother Doerfelt was dug up. I remember clearly how we inspected the bones as they were shoveled out of the ground and thinking this was my Great-Grandmother's body. Surprisingly, I was not at all spooked or uncomfortable. I had spent many hours with my Great-Grandmother Doerfelt as a child and loved listening to her stories. She was my grandmother's mother and lived until she was quite old.

Our Church had a large bell tower and the huge bells were rung with an attached rope. It was the job and the responsibility of the young teens in Church to ring the bells at the appropriate time of the day on weekends and when school was out. I loved ringing the bells, they were so heavy though that I often was lifted up off the floor and had quite a time ringing the bell that was assigned to me smoothly without jerking the rope.

* * *

The first family tragedy happened shortly after the war started. My Aunt Selmel (one of Papa's sisters) died suddenly. She, along with my Aunt Marthel, took some cooking classes to learn how to prepare fish. Later that evening Aunt Selmel became quite ill. The doctor was summoned, but he thought it was a case of the flu. Later in the day she died of fish poisoning. She was only 39 years old and the mother of my good friend and cousin Inge. The whole family was devastated. Inge and her little brother was so sad when their mother died and I grieved along with them. Inge was my soul mate and I loved her dearly. After Inge's mother died, she came to live with us for a year and when her father remarried she moved back to be with her father and stepmother. Inge was truly like a sister to me.

I remember so clearly that Grandmother prayed with us every morning before we went to school. What a wonderful custom...

* * *

Growing up in "Hitler's Germany" was often difficult. I belonged to the Hitler Youth, a youth organization much like Boy Scouts or Girl Scouts, and have many fond memories of hiking in the hills, singing, doing crafts and other fun-activities. There was one exception. We were taught to love The Fuehrer and to be loyal to the Homeland. Our meetings always started with a lesson on politics and current events. Singing "Hitler's Songs" and marching in long lines up and down the main street of our village was an activity always scheduled for Sunday mornings. As the years went by, all rallies and meetings were held on Sunday mornings, preventing the children and youth from attending church services. Unless we had a very valid excuse, we were expected to attend all meetings and functions of the Hitler Youth. Membership of the Hitler Youth was not voluntary. A child automatically was enrolled upon entering school. All of my cousins and friends belonged to the Hitler Youth and participated in all aspects of that organization.

My father had four brothers Walter, Martin, Johannes and Erich. Walter and Erich lived in Zschorlau, too. Martin lived in northern Germany and Johannes lived in Duesseldorf, on the Rhein. Walter and his wife Elli had one daughter, Christa. She was a few years older than I was and was very pretty. I looked up to her and was always glad when she played with me, or when I was able to spend some time with her. Erich's wife was named Marthel, as was Papa's youngest sister. They had one daughter whose name was Rita. She was several years younger than I was.

Martin and his wife Elfriede had no children. He was my very favorite uncle and I adored him. He made me feel very special when I was with him. All of my other uncles had their own children, but Martin had no children of his own and therefore spent a lot of time with me when he was visiting his parents and family in Zschorlau. His nickname for me was "maus." In my estimation he was a very good-looking and a dashing man. He often said that he kept his slim figure because he stopped eating when it tasted the best. In those days that was quite a revolutionary idea.

* * *

My uncle Johannes was married to a very beautiful lady. Her name was Grete. They had a son and a daughter and I loved them both a lot. Unfortunately I did not get to see them too often at the beginning of the war.

During all of my growing up years we never went on a trip or took a vacation. The financial situation of my grandparents, as well as the declining health of my grandmother, did not allow for any luxuries. Although my grandparents were on a very limited income, money was never discussed and I always had what I needed.

* * *

Martin and Johannes were both chosen to be in the S.S., which was the elite of the Military. It was an honor and quite an achievement to become an S.S. man. My grandparents were very proud of them. Erich was drafted into the Infantry.

* * *

Papa had three sisters left after Selmel died. Anna Anger, Hedwig Richter and Marthel Wilhelm. Marthel was like my older sister. She was still living at home while I was a little girl and we spent a lot of time together. She was a very fun-loving young woman and took care of me much of the time, especially when my grandmother was ill. One day, my school class was going on a field trip and many of the mothers of my school friends went along. I asked my Aunt Marthel if she would pretend to be my Mother for the day. I wanted a young mother, too.

* * *

Marthel married Hans Siegel shortly after Selmel died. The two sisters had been very close and I remember them coming home from a shopping trip to Aue where they had purchased Marthel's wedding gown. It was such a happy day for them, as they talked about the upcoming wedding. When Selmel died a short time later, Marthel traded the wedding dress in for a black mourning dress. She wore that dress at her wedding. At that time it was still the tradition for ladies to wear black clothes and for men to wear black armbands on their coat sleeves for a full year after a death occurred in the family. For several years it seemed that our family wore black continuously. Shortly after Marthel and Hans's daughter Thea was born, he too had to go off to war. He was the first uncle to be killed in action. Marthel was a young widow with an adorable little girl. Again, they moved back in with my grandparents.

And the war raged on...

* * *

Every home in Germany was expected to display a picture of the Fuehrer in a prominent place. Ours was a large picture of Hitler, hanging in my grandparents' bedroom. One day when I came home from school, the picture was gone. In dismay, I asked my grandfather, "What happened to the Fuehrer's picture?"

His reply was, " I will not have a picture of this man in my home any longer".

I was absolutely stunned. How could he say a thing like that about MY FUEHRER, who was so wonderful? After all, that is what we were taught in our Hitler Youth classes. I almost turned my beloved grandfather in to the authorities. That is how strongly I felt about the situation and how brainwashed I was, even as a young child.

The school I attended was only 2 blocks away from home and was a beautiful modern building. I really liked going to school and did quite well. My grades were good, but I could have studied harder to excel. My grandparents were never too strict about my schoolwork, but kept in close touch with my teachers. My favorite subjects were reading and history.

Summer vacations from school were always a time I looked forward to with great anticipation. Swimming pools were closed during the war to conserve water, neither were any teachers for swimming classes available and I had no opportunity to learn how to swim. A popular recreational spot and lake in our area was a lake called "Filzteich" that Inge and I went to at times, that is, if one of the aunts or other adults accompanied us. We had to walk about one hour to get to the lake, but it was a great outing for us. I remember one summer when my sister Eva came to visit us in Zschorlau we went to the Filzteich to go swimming and have a picnic. Eva was a competent swimmer and encouraged me to go in the water with her. We were playing around and she threw me into the deep water, not realizing that I did not know how to swim. I was struggling to get back into the shallower area of the lake, sputtering and splashing all the way. It was a very scary experience for me and it took me a long time to get over being frightened and to get back into the water of a lake or swimming pool.

* * *

Back to China... The Wilhelm's enjoyed several years of unhindered ministry in Hunan when a grave famine hit the province. They then suffered the consequences of the Japanese invasion and war with China, which began in July of 1937. The same year the

Wilhelm's were blessed with their sixth child: Margarethe Edelgard.

With the approach of the Japanese armed forces and air raids and bombing attacks, life for my family, as well as all of the missionary families who lived in China, became more and more difficult.

* * *

After Pearl Harbor in December of 1941, Germany entered into a state of war with China due to its alliance with Japan and Italy. A number of German missionaries, including my family, were placed under house arrest and on January 27,1942, they entered a Chinese concentration camp shared with other German and Italian aliens.

By God's grace they finally were able to obtain permission to leave the Interior of China. Under police and military escort they were brought to the border of French Indochina (North Vietnam) and officially expelled from China. From there they made their way up north to Shanghai, now under Japanese occupation, and re-entered China in June 1942. There my father served for six years as pastor of the German Lutheran Church. The communist take-over of China led to the withdrawal and exodus of the foreign community, eventually including all missionaries.

* * *

In the spring of 1941 we received word from the Liebenzell Mission that my oldest Sister Eva, (called Evchen by the family) was returning to Germany. She was to continue her schooling, since she had reached the end of her sixth grade, the final year of the missionary school. Eva, as well as my other siblings in China, went to a missionary boarding school, being separated from their parents during the school year, except for vacations.

* * *

Eva was able to get out of China, via Russia, on a children's transport program, the last one being offered before the war between Russia and Germany broke out.

I was so excited about the prospect of seeing my oldest sister and being with her. I could hardly sleep at night any more in anticipation of Evchen's arrival. The day of her arrival I scrubbed our kitchen floor with such vigor; I wanted to make sure that everything was spotless for my sister. I doubt that she even noticed the floor.

When I think of the time when I first met Evchen, I remember that I looked at her awe inspired. She had come from so far and had traveled such a long distance. I adored her, although I do not remember having any conversations with her about China, or the family. I am sure that she must have told me things about our parents and the other siblings. I just do not recall what she said, or told me. She must have been terribly homesick, being in a strange country with strange people. A nine-year-old little girl who was a sister she didn't know, and grandparents who her sister called "Mother" and "Father" must have been strange and confusing.

Evchen had seen many countries and places in her young life and had so many experiences that were overwhelming to me. I had not even been outside of Sachsen, our home state. She talked about going to the mountains in the summer with the family and staying in a little house that they called "The Anita House." They named a house after me, so they must have thought of me and remembered me.

I still remember the certain odor that I called "the Chinese odor" that permeated around her fabric-lined suitcase when she opened it and unpacked. To this day, anything that comes from China has the same odor to me. Unfortunately, Eva was in Zschorlau only for a very short time.

She was to live in Muellheim, Baden, at the Mission's Children's Home, where she got her education. Muellheim was in southern Germany. Former Liebenzell Missionaries Tante and Onkel Grohmann ran the children's home. So again, we were separated. She came to visit us in Zschorlau once during the summer over school vacation. Eva and I got along quite well and I loved being with her.

* * *

Further tragedy struck the Wilhelm family in 1943 when my dear, dear Uncle Martin was killed in action in Russia. It was the first real personal sorrow that I felt in my childhood. I loved Uncle Martin so much. I remember so well what happened a few weeks prior to his death. Martin was stationed in Prague, Czechoslovakia. The part of Germany where I grew up, "the Erzgebirge" (translated "the Ore Mountain"), is located just north of the Czech border. Martin often came home to visit his parents on a short furlough. I always loved it when he came. That particular time when he came to visit, he was not at all himself. He seemed unhappy and depressed. My Grandmother took him aside and asked him what was troubling him. She was very concerned about him. I was in the next room and inadvertently overheard the conversation that transpired between mother and son. But I did not fully understand the meaning of what was said until much later. He said, "Mother, I have to do things and perform certain acts that are totally against anything I believe in. It goes against my Christian upbringing as well as my moral integrity. But I have no choice but to follow orders. If I am insubordinate to my orders I, as well as my whole Company of men, would very likely be shipped to the front." And the war front was in Russia. Two weeks later he notified us that his whole troop was being ordered to the front. It was shortly thereafter that the military telegram arrived with the news that S.S Officer Martin Wilhelm was missing in action and presumed dead. The location where he was last seen and heard of was close to Moscow. The German soldiers could not survive the harsh Russian winter as well as the over-powering Russian military forces. Thousands of lives were lost.

Later, after the war had ended and the truth of the atrocities of the Jewish extermination became known, Martin's words became clear to us. He most likely was involved with Jews and one of the war camps. How tragically it all ended!

This photo of my Uncle Martin (officer on right) was taken in February 1942 near Moscow.

The last letter I received from Uncle Martin, with the English translation below

My Dear Mouse!
Many thanks for your dear letter from August 24, 1943. I am always so happy when I receive mail from you. Continue to do well in school and work hard, in school as well as at home, helping your grandmother. I want to only hear good things about you when I come home on furlough. Greetings to all of the loved ones at home, but special greetings to you.

From Your Martin

5

"Das Silberne Erzgebirge" The Silver Erzgebirge

The Erzgebirge, translated "Ore Mountains," is a small mountainous range in the southeastern part of the State of Sachsen in eastern Germany. The heavily forested chain of mountains with picturesque and ever-changing landscape is one of Germany's most beautiful spots. Its many mines are rich in uranium, silver, iron and cobalt. Little forgotten and sleepy simple villages nestled in the valleys, surrounded by soft rolling hills. My hometown Zschorlau was one of these villages.

The Erzgebirge is also rich in tradition and folklore, and best known for its woodcarvings, wooden toy manufacturing and Kloeppeln (lace making). Many folk songs are written about the beautiful and much beloved Erzgebirge in its own "erzgebirgisch dialect". The language might be hard for outsiders to understand, but for people who live there, it is part of their heritage. Children in school are taught High German, the correct spoken and written German language, but at home and among themselves "erzgebirgisch" is the common language spoken. I loved it!

* * *

Winter, with its pure-white cover of snow, came early to the mountains, much sooner then in the flatland of Germany. The rolling hills were wonderful for sledding, skiing and playing in the snow. We bundled up very warmly and off we went. I did not have far to go to either do some sledding down the hill close to where I lived, or to put on my skis and take off. Oh, how I loved being outdoors, playing in the snow. There were no ski lifts, we walked up the hill on skis and skied down the hill, over and over. What fun that was! One day, some of the boys I was skiing with dared me to ski through one of the little wooded areas, and of course I did. I took quite a spill when I hit a snow covered tree stump, cutting a long gash in my leg. I tried to ignore it, until I saw blood oozing out from under my ski-pants. I was afraid to go home and confess my folly for fear that I would get a good scolding. True to my fears, I got quite a scolding.

6

Christmas in the Erzgebirg Mountains

Of old, "das Erzgebirge" was labeled "the German Christmas country," and rightfully so. Sooner than anywhere else in the country, the snowed-in little villages and mountain towns started to prepare for Christmas. It was my favorite time of the year. Although gift-giving and often the traditional food for Christmas was at a minimum during the war-years, our other traditions made Christmas a Celebration of Christ's Birthday, Lights and Joy.

A town square in Erzgebirg at Christmas time

* * *

The celebration started with the first of Advent, when the first candle on the Advent wreath was lit. What a special time of anticipation and excitement it was! All four Advent Sundays were days of celebration, until finally, Christmas was near.

All of our Christmas decorations were brought out and unpacked and lovingly put in their right place. There were Miners with candles, Angels with Candles, Pyramids, Nutcrackers and Smokers. I can still remember the balsam odor of the incense that the little Smoker men puffed out of their mouths. It was all so awesome.

The Christmas "Stollen" was baked in every home and bakery, as well as special cookies and Pfefferkuchen. Oh, how good they smelled.

The Christmas tree was a special gift for the family. I was never allowed to see it until after we returned home from our church service on Christmas Eve. It was Grandfather's job to decorate the tree on Christmas Eve day and once the tree entered our parlor, no one was allowed in the room. From that moment on, it became the Christmas room. Every person in the family had a special little table of their own. It was laden with unwrapped gifts, fruit and cookies. That part of the tradition was Grandmother's job. Roast goose, red cabbage and potato dumplings made our special traditional feast on Christmas Eve. After dinner, we attended church services and when we arrived back home we were invited into the Christmas room. The candles on the tree shone brightly, and under the tree, very prominently, Grandfather had placed the Nativity scene. Jesus was the real gift of Christmas.

* * *

On Christmas morning we had a special Service in Church called "the Metten". It was a wonderful service with lots of music and candlelight. The service started at 6 o'clock in the morning. The crunching sound that our shoes made on the snow as we walked to Church still rings in my ears. It was still dark out and seemed like the middle of the night. As we approached the Church, we could hear the wondrous sound of a brass choir playing Christmas carols in front of the Church. It was awe-inspiring! The big pipe organ inside the Church was playing as we entered God's house. On each side of the Altar stood a huge Christmas tree, decorated with white paper stars and white candles. It was a tradition for the children of the church to make the paper stars several weeks before Christmas on special Sunday afternoons. The trees were so beautiful in their simplicity.

* * *

After Church as we walked back home, we watched the window displays in the houses we passed by. We always knew how many girls and boys lived in a house. When a boy child was born into a family, he received the traditional carved Miner. A girl child received the traditional carved Angel. The statues held candles. The Miners and Angels were placed in the windows and the candles were lit, and everyone knew how many children lived in a house. When we arrived home, it was time to gather with the whole family and serve the Christmas Stollen that was never cut into before Christmas. Oh, the memories of Christmases gone by!

I remember one Christmas with regrets. It was Christmas Eve afternoon and I was so anxious to find out what I might be getting for a gift that I peaked into the room through the keyhole. I saw a beautiful doll buggy with the most precious doll I had ever seen, which was to be mine. I was so excited, but felt so guilty that I had seen my wonderful present, before I was supposed to see it. It almost spoiled Christmas for me. It taught me a very valuable lesson.

7
The War Continues...

Living in a small village, in a relatively remote part of the country, was quite advantageous during the war. Unlike the industrial cities and areas of Germany, especially the ones that produced ammunition and war related products, the region where I grew up was not a target for heavy bombings. Even though we did not experience actual bombings, planes flew over us almost every night, and we spent many nights in bomb shelters. Our bomb shelter was in the cellar of the house we lived in. When the bomb-sirens went off, we had to get up, get dressed and hurry into the cellar. We often stayed there for hours, until the sirens went off again in a different sound to notify us that the alert was over. If we had to stay up until after 2 a.m. in the morning, we did not have school the next day, or had classes in the afternoon only. There were isolated bombings in our area, but the real destruction from the bombing was directed to large cities. The Rheinland, especially the Ruhr-area with its highly industrial cities, was the target for destruction. Windows in every home were required to have blackout shades and heavy fines were imposed for any violations.

Not only did we have to cope with the almost nightly air raids, but we also had a shortage of food and everything from food to shoes and clothing was rationed. We had food stamps that were treasured like pieces of gold. I do not remember ever not having a meal during the war, though, the kind of food was not always our choice, or to our liking. But it kept us fed. Fruit was hardly ever available. I remember one Christmas we were given two oranges for the whole family. We shared them, savoring every bite.

In 1944, the French were attacking the town of Muellheim, where my sister Eva lived, and my grandparents insisted that Eva should be sent to Zschorlau because it was too dangerous for her to remain in Muellheim. She was forced to flee Muellheim in the middle of the night, getting on a train that was heading east. Her ultimate destination was Zschorlau. I have few memories of that time. Eva went to school in Aue and I remember her bringing a refugee girl home to study.

* * *

The year was 1945 when Dresden was almost totally destroyed in a bombing attack by Allied British Bombers. That night will always stand out in my memory. We stayed in the cellar (that was our bomb-shelter) most of the night and when we were able to come up and go outside the whole firmament was red from the reflection of the fires in Dresden. It was awesome, frightening and devastating.

Dresden is the Capital of Sachsen and is about 80 miles from my hometown. It was one of Europe's foremost cultural centers before World War II. In one night, the 18th century Zwinger Palace with wonderful Museums, the State Opera House, the Hofkirche, as well as the Kreuzkirche that in part dates from the 15th Century were destroyed. German Culture at its best was gone.

Many of the families who lived in the war and bomb stricken cities and areas came to our area as refugees, because it was much safer to live in smaller communities.

* * *

My uncle Johannes, Joh for short, who was a brother of my father, lived in Duesseldorf with his wife and two children, Horst and Fee. Joh was also an S.S. Officer, like my uncle Martin, serving his country in the war. My Aunt Grete and her children came to Zschorlau every year to get a reprieve from the bombings. I was always happy when Horst and Fee came. I loved being with them. They brought a bit of "City" to our small village and seemed so sophisticated even as children.

Uncle Joh and Tante Grete owned a big furniture store in Duesseldorf. On one of their visits with us, they were notified that their store as well as their home had been destroyed in a bombing attack. It was a very sad time for them. Tante Grete's mother was Jewish and it is still a puzzle to me that she did not fall into the hands of the Nazis. Her name was Frau Roehrig and she often came to Zschorlau along with Tante Grete and her children.

Shortly before the war ended, Uncle Joh and his command were stationed in the very western part of Germany defending their country to the end. It was there that, one night as he was walking toward the quarters where he lived, he was shot from a sniper who was hiding in a tree. My Aunt Grete and Aunt Marthel took the train from Zschorlau to the town where Joh was lying near death in a field hospital. He had a severe head injury and died shortly thereafter.

Again, my grandparents lost a son.

My uncle Walter and his family lived in Zschorlau. He served his country during the First World War and lost a leg. Therefore he was exempt from the Military during World War II. However, he was a Director in a Refuge-Camp in Erfurt, which was in a neighboring state of Sachsen. His wife Eli and daughter Christa lived in Zschorlau during that time and only saw Walter on occasions.

At the end of the war, word arrived from Russia that my Uncle Erich, the youngest of Papa's brothers, was a prisoner of war in Russia. Needless to say, this was a very, very sad time for the whole family.

The war came closer to home and air raids were almost an every night occurrence. The bombings of Leipzig and Dresden, the two main cities of Sachsen were dreadful and in Dresden alone 135,000 people were killed.

During the war years we had little contact with my parents in China. Our only communications were 25 word telegrams that we received every few months, and then we returned a 25-word message. Many of them contained news of another loss in the family. Towards the end of the war, we had no contact with my family in China at all and did not know if they were alive or dead.

In the meantime, my family in China had to endure many hardships as well. They had to leave their mission-station in the interior of China and after being placed in different camps ended up in Shanghai. The year was 1942. At that time, Shanghai was considered to be the largest city in China with an enormous population of foreigners.

While in Shanghai, Papa and Mutti were associated with The China Inland Mission and the family lived at the compound of the CIM. Papa was the Mission's Transport Manager and was responsible for making travel arrangements for the incoming and outgoing missionaries.

My two sisters and two brothers were enrolled in a German school in Shanghai to receive their education.

In 1944 Papa became the pastor of the German Lutheran Church in Shanghai, a position he held until 1950 when the communists forced all foreigners, including my family, out of China.

* * *

At the end of the war many people who were living in the eastern states of Germany had to flee the Russians and were driven westward. Trains were overloaded with refugees and looked like cattle trains. Long trains of refugees, carrying their meager belongings behind them, came through Zschorlau.

Also, whole troops of German solders, tired and in rags marched through our village. One of them was Hubert Kariger, who stayed and later became the husband of Marthel.

We heard the rumbling artillery of the advancing American Army forces daily and were so frightened. 55 years later we learned that a good friend from Scottsbluff was wounded while advancing on a town close to my home. In 1998 he and his wife revisited the area and also went through Zschorlau, my hometown.

People living in our village and surrounding areas were asked to take in as many refuges as they were able to house. At times we had 3 or 4 people living with us. Our parlor became a makeshift bedroom and our limited amounts of food were shared. Some of the refugees stayed with us only a short time, others stayed longer. I do not know where they all went, but they all traveled west.

* * *

The real true followers of Adolf Hitler still believed that he had one last great plan to save Germany from losing the war. I remember sitting on the front step of our house when one of our neighbors, Frau Bochroeder, came to sit beside me. She was crying. She loved Adolf

Hitler and truly believed that he would save us from the Americans and the Russians. She was totally destroyed when we heard the news that Adolf Hitler had killed himself, and that it was all over. Germany surrendered on May 7th, 1945.

The war had come to an end, and Germany was conquered.

I was fourteen years old...

8
The Post War Years...

The next few years that followed are a blur to me. It is as if I blocked some of the experiences from my mind.

The general feeling was chaos everywhere...

Shortly after the war ended, we were told that the Americans were occupying our part of the country and we were so happy. I remember standing on the side of the road as trucks and jeeps loaded with solders rolled along the main street of Zschorlau. The soldiers seemed friendly enough and waved at us, even threw candy bars to the children. Unfortunately, the Americans did not stay very long and soon left the same way they arrived.

* * *

When World War II ended in 1945, leaders from US, Britain and USSR met at the Potsdam Conference. They decided to temporarily divide Germany into four occupation zones. French in the Southwest, British in the northwest, American in the south, and Soviet in the east. That decision was a slow death for Eastern

Germany. We were to be occupied by the Soviets. It was a real tragedy for all of us.

Soon after the Americans departed, the Russians entered our village. The difference between the Americans and the Russians was indescribable. I remember the curfews, the large army trucks and tanks rolling into our town and tearing up the streets, the unruly and intoxicated Russian soldiers and the frightened residents of the homes and towns. So much happened in the next months and years!

The Russians took over homes and any buildings that pleased them and that they wanted. They invaded all privacy, breaking into homes and raping women, old and young alike, including nuns. Seven soldiers lived in our house, using every available room, as well as the kitchen facilities. I must say that for the most part they were considerate of my grandmother who was ill and they left us to ourselves. But we were always frightened when they tried to get into our apartment late at night, especially when they were drunk. One night while Eva and I were sleeping, a very intoxicated soldier by the name of Alec was pounding on our door trying to get in. We huddled together, hoping and praying that he wouldn't break the door in. He left very angry and in his stupor fell down a flight of stairs. The next morning when we saw him he had two black eyes and had also been reprimanded by his superior officer who had heard the ruckus during the night.

Another day the same soldier, Alec, brought us a chicken that he had stolen from a nearby farmyard. He felt sorry for the sick grandmother and wanted to do something special for her.

During that time our food-supply was extremely scarce, much worse than during the war years. We hungered and it seemed that our thoughts primarily centered on food.

My Aunt Marthel, who had been living with us, married Hubert Kariger and moved into her own apartment. Eva was in charge of the household and worked very hard. Mother had rheumatism and was not able to do anything but sit.

We had very little to eat, - a few potatoes and a little bread and not much more. In the morning we would go to the meadows and gather some sort of wild spinach leaves that we made a soup out of by adding a grated potato to thicken the green gruel. It was not good, but filled our stomachs to some extent. Every person in the household was given a portion of bread for the week. Woe if someone else took a bit of your bread. Salt was also unavailable. We used some sort of a substitute. I remember a day when we sat down for a meal of the green gruel and Grandfather took one bite and pushed his plate to the side, saying, "I can not eat this." It was cooked without salt and tasted horrible. A few times we heard of horsemeat being sold in a butcher shop. We stood in line for hours to purchase a piece of that advertised meat. It tasted very sweet and was stringy, but it was meat.

* * *

The cook for the Russians who were living in our house cooked wonderful meals for them and the cooking odors permeated throughout the house. We were so envious and would have loved some of their leftover food, but the cleaning crew mixed their leftover food with garbage.

Many stories circulated about the Russians. The ones who were occupying Zschorlau were a very tough and uneducated lot and most of them were illiterate. We heard that at the end of the war Russia opened up its prisons to increase their military force. I believe it.

One soldier was killed right in front of our eyes. He stole a bicycle and rode down the hill of our little brick road, ended up across the street smashing into a brick wall of a house. He had never ridden a bicycle before.

They all loved watches and stole them from everyone in sight who was wearing them. It was common to see the soldiers wearing several wristwatches on their arm. Sometimes the whole arm was covered with watches. The story was told about a soldier carrying a big alarm clock around his neck on a chain. The alarm clock was an old-fashioned one - the kind that had a bell on top. When it started ringing, he tore it off his neck, threw it to the ground and shot it to pieces, running up and down the street, screaming, "The Devil is in this thing"

It seemed that the Russians were in our house for quite some time, but I don't exactly recall how long.

After the war our church congregation was blessed with a new Pastor whose name was Pfarrer (Pastor) Froehlich. He was a refugee driven out of his home state of Schlesien (a state in east Germany). I remember him as a very gentle and wonderful person, as well as a very caring Pastor.

He brought his ailing wife and daughter Angelika with him who was very helpful with the young people in church. She was the epitome of a minister's daughter in my eyes and I really admired her.

During the war, all the state churches had ministers who were called "Deutsche Christen" (German Christians). They were far from what we understand as a Christian and they certainly did not preach the gospel. The Nazi pastors were preaching politics and Adolf Hitler from the Chancel and raised their arm in a "Heil Hitler" salute when the church service started.

Reverend Boehm, the Nazi minister, left our church in Zschorlau immediately when the Hitler regime failed.

As was the custom, the children in church started confirmation classes when they reached the age of fourteen. Our new pastor started my Confirmation Class in 1946, and that was the year that I was confirmed. Confirmation was a big event and an important celebration in a young person's life and I took the commitment I made to the Church and God very seriously!

Inge and I were confirmed together. We were still very close and shared so much that was happening in our lives.

It was so important to have the right wardrobe for Confirmation. Although dresses and fabrics were very hard to come by, somehow I got two new dresses. There was of course the black dress for the Church ceremony itself and another one; mine was wine-red, for the celebration later at home and with friends. I was so proud of my new dresses. They were especially made for me and were beautiful. But I had a dilemma, no shoes. That was a commodity that was very hard to come by. Most of the shoes we wore were made of see-through plastic and that just would not do for confirmation. My Grandfather came to the rescue. He had a friend in Aue who was a shoemaker and that is who we were going visit. I do not remember his name, but I can still visualize his shoe store and shop where he showed us a piece of gray leather that he was going to use for my new shoes. He took careful measurements of my feet and promised to have them ready for the big occasion.

And he fulfilled his promise. Grandfather very proudly presented me with my new pair of shoes. I remember exactly what they looked like, however the left shoe was quite a bit smaller than the right shoe. I was heartbroken, but did not have the heart to admit to my Grandfather that my new shoes hurt my feet. He was so proud of my new shoes. I wore them for a long time.

* * *

That same year the children and the young people in Church presented a Passion Play on Christmas. I was the Angel Gabriel and had to sing a solo. The Minister came up to me afterwards and told me how well I did. That made me feel so good.

In 1946 I finished my schooling in Zschorlau and that Fall started going to school in Aue. Aue was the largest town in our district and about 5-6 miles from Zschorlau.

I was enrolled in a "home-economics school" for girls my age. It was in preparation for the school that I wanted to attend in Zwickau later on.

The school in Aue was for one year. I did well in school and really liked it. It was quite a challenge for the teacher of my cooking class to teach us how to cook when we had no food to cook with! We learned everything theoretically and did a lot of experimenting using food substitutes. I made new friends and liked my new surroundings. To get to school I either went by bus, walked, or in the winter when we had snow, I used my skis.

* * *

It was during that time that my Uncle Erich returned from his imprisonment in Russia. He looked like an old man. He was emaciated, starved, and nothing but skin and bones.

It was shocking for us to see him like that, but he certainly was not the only soldier who came back in that condition. The certainty was that he did come back from the war, unlike his two brothers Martin and Joh, as well as his brother-in-law Hans Siegel. The whole family was so happy to welcome him back home, especially Grandmother, who was still grieving for her fallen sons. I do not think she ever coped with the loss of her children and I am convinced that, at the end, she died of a broken heart.

Many evenings I remember Erich coming to visit us after he had dinner with his family to eat what we had saved for him from our meager dinner. From our house he went to visit the other relatives who lived in Zschorlau. He was so starved and we all were happy to share what little food we had with him.

It was during the worst time of our lives when we thought we would surely starve to death that my parents in China found a way to send us some *care packages* via missionary friends from all over. Missionaries helped by my father in China were now helping us by sending food, as well as clothing. The packages came from Switzerland and other countries. Oh, how welcome they were and such a godsend! All of a sudden we had white flour and fat, coffee and cocoa and all sorts of other food we had not seen in years. We traded some of the coffee in for bread and butter from farmers who had a better food supply than we did. I remember Eva and I eating some of the fatty foods and since our stomachs had not been used to good food, it made us sick. But it surely tasted good!

Some of the packages also contained used clothing that was in good condition. I recall that we got a large package in the mail one day and when we opened it, it contained an old army coat. How disappointing that was to us. Evidently someone had stolen the contents of the package and replaced them with the old coat.

Often clothes that were sent did not fit us properly and we shared them with relatives or friends. These care packages literally saved us from starvation and gave us such encouragement to struggle on in this horrendous economic post war struggle. We were so thankful to my parents and the friends who so lovingly and generously helped us in our time of need.

My Grandparents were very strict and fundamentally religious and did not believe in dancing, playing cards, or going to a movie or a play. Eva and I were in our teens and often would have liked to do these "worldly things," but got into utter disgrace with the grandparents if we went to a movie or a play against their wishes. One time we did go to Aue to a play that we really wanted to see, but it was considered very sinful in the eyes of our grandparents.

In the fall of 1947, I moved to Zwickau, a city of east central Germany, in Sachsen where I was accepted to a private Women's College called "Frauenfachschule." The school was one of the better-known schools in our area, specializing in home economics. That field had always been of interest to me and I was excited to have the opportunity to continue my education. Zwickau was about 50 miles away from home and was an industrial center located in a coal-mining region.

I recall that my Uncle Walter moved me to Zwickau on the 6th of September 1947 and after he had situated me in my dormitory, he left me to my own devices. None of the other girls had moved in yet and I was alone in the house, except for my dorm mother who was too busy to pay much attention to me. I remember walking through the streets of Zwickau sobbing; I felt so lonely and forlorn. As time went on, I made good friends and enjoyed my stay at the dorm and I liked my classes in school. I spent most of my weekends at home in Zschorlau. Often when I returned on Monday I brought some special treats that came from one of the care-packages and I shared them with some of my friends at school. I became popular quickly and often wondered if it was me my new friends liked, or my treats that I brought from home.

My school and the adjacent dormitory were located on the Ring, a circular street in Zwickau, behind the 15th Century Church of St.Mary, a German Gothic structure that ranks among one of the finest in Germany. Right next to the Cathedral stood the birth-house of German Composer Robert Schumann. I often visited the house that was made into a Museum and displayed much of Schumann's memorabilia, as well as that of his wife Clara, who was a well-known pianist in Germany before she married Robert Schumann. It was so intriguing for me to learn all about this man and woman whom I admired so much. I loved Schumann's "Traeumerei " that he wrote especially for his wife and envisioned her sitting close to the piano, swooning over him and listening to that lovely melody. It was all so romantic.

My first year in school went very well and I decided to take classes in special diets. I was also interested in all of my sewing and design classes. I did well in school and enjoyed living in a city. Some of our special assignments were reports of theater productions, operas and operettas. The theatre was not too far from school and it was great to be able to attend these functions without feeling guilty and sinful.

The "Frauenfachschule" was a three-year program, which consisted of classes for the first year, a "practicum" for the second year and classes for the third year. My first year ended on the 23rd of July 1948

* * *

In June of 1948, Eva left Zschorlau to go back to Muellheim. She was able to get out of Russian Germany because she had lived in West Germany before the war ended.

I was sad to see my sister leave again, but I understood that she had no future in Zschorlau and desperately wanted to move back to the West.

* * *

My assignment for my yearlong practicum was a Motherhouse for Deaconesses of the Evangelical Lutheran church called: "Zion." It was located on the outskirts of Aue in a very beautiful park-like setting, very inviting and peaceful. I was assigned to work in all the different departments of the institution, such as the kitchen, dining room, laundry facility and the gardens to get hands-on experience in a large-scale domestic environment. I learned a lot from the Sisters (that was the name given to the Deaconesses) while I was there, but it was not a very exciting time of my life. The work was tedious and the atmosphere was very stiff and structured. There were several other girls there working with me who were not in training to become a deaconess.

My Grandmother died on September 29, 1948. Although Mother had been ill for years, it was still a terrible shock to me when she died. I was heartbroken. Again, I was left behind.

I was living in Aue at the time and was called home to be with Mother in her last hours. I remember just taking off from the Motherhouse without permission walking and running to Zschorlau. It normally took me about one hour to walk home, but this time I arrived there much quicker. I remember Mother lying in bed with Father, and several of the aunts and uncles surrounding her. She was failing fast and it was the first time that I actually saw someone dying. I think she was semi-conscious when I arrived but I was convinced that she knew that I was there. She died a short time later.

I was devastated and felt a real depth of grief and loss. My grandmother was the only Mother I had known in my life and I loved her dearly.

In my despair I wrote many letters to my parents, looking for guidance and especially comfort for my stricken soul. Papa was mourning himself over the loss of his Mother whom he had not seen in 14 years. His letters to me were outlined with many scripture verses and generic comforting phrases. It was not what I wanted and I was feeling very lonely and motherless. But how could he comfort his daughter who mourned the loss of her Mother who was in reality HIS Mother? There must have been a real conflict of feelings at this time for him that was hard to explain or describe. After a few months, he simply said that I needed to get over my grieving and get on with it.

Maybe that was the answer I needed, but at the time the reality of my situation became clear, I had to be independent and live my life the best I could.

The last year of my education in Zwickau was from 1949 to 1950. For the most part that was a good year for me. I felt less isolated in the dorm and had many friends. School was going well and I enjoyed my classes. I was going out on dates on occasion and my own sense of myself was beginning to improve and I felt an increase of self- confidence.

The economic conditions were still bad, but somehow we coped with the situation.

There was a tremendous housing shortage in Eastern Germany after the war and my hometown of Zschorlau was not spared. Families had to share their homes with other family members. So it came to pass that after Grandmother died, my Aunt Annel who was widowed, gave up her apartment and moved in with my Grandfather.

She had two sons, Lothar and Gerd. Lothar was one year older than I was and Gerd was several years younger. My home became their home.

The first time I came home from school for the weekend, I had the greatest shock of my life. All of the furniture that had belonged to my grandparents had been removed and had been replaced with my Aunt's belongings. My Grandfather had been moved into a little attic room that I used as a playroom in my childhood. My home had disappeared!!! I could not bear to stay there for the weekend. I turned around, left the old Bochmann house, and took the first train back to Zwickau to my dorm. I was heartsick and felt so forlorn and homeless. My self-confidence was shot down once more.

After that episode I often took the train to Schlema, another town near my hometown, where the Richter family resided. My Aunt Hedwig was one of Papa's sisters and was married to Max Richter. They had 6 children, 5 sons and one daughter, my cousins. Two of the sons were slightly older than I was and the other three sons and the daughter were younger than I was. I felt very comfortable with the Richters and was always welcome at their home. Their small house was very modest and they lived very conservatively, but their home was full of love and contentment. My aunt and uncle had always been close friends of my parents and therefore felt a special kinship to me.

This was during the time that the Russian soldiers were roaming the streets of every town and village and were often uncontrollable. I remember so well how protective my cousins were of me when I had to walk to the train station early on Monday mornings to return to school at Zwickau. They took turns accompanying me to the train station very early in the morning and stayed with me until my train arrived and I was safely settled in one of the train's compartments. I have never forgotten their concern and love for me. I was truly blessed to be able to lean on and spend my free time with that wonderful family. They were a real comfort haven for me and I will be forever grateful to the Richter family.

9
Exit from China

The following is an excerpt from the Biographical Sketch of my father, Karl Max Wilhelm:

> *Brother Wilhelm served as pastor of the German Lutheran Church in Shanghai from 1944 until 1950. The Wilhelm's made their exodus from China in the spring of 1950 with the last available American ship. They made the difficult choice of starting a new life in the United States, rather than returning to their home country of Germany. This was largely due to provide for the educational needs of their children, the present economic needs of post-war Germany and the hope of bringing about a reunion of their family. The Wilhelm's arrived in California on May 23 of 1950.*

* * *

It was in the spring of 1950 that I finished my schooling in the "Frauenfachschule" in Zwickau and after successfully completing and passing the required exams, graduated with the class of 1950. F.F.II was the last class allowed to finish their education before the school was closed by the Communist Government in East Germany due to the fact that it was a private school and therefore not in compliance with Communist regulations and doctrines. It was a bittersweet graduation, knowing that the old established school for young women would have to close its doors forever. Saying "Goodbye" to all of my friends was hard, knowing that I would perhaps never see them again.

It was during that difficult time that I received a letter from my parents in China with the news that they were re-locating in the United States instead of coming back to Germany, an event that I had often dreamed of. The letter also stated that my parents wanted for my sister Eva and me to come to the United States as well, so that we could be re-united as a family.

10
Farewell

It was a very difficult decision for me to make. I felt such loyalty to my Germany! Times were tough, but Germany was my home and I did not want to leave a sinking ship. However, the strong urge that was within me to finally meet my parents and siblings and the responsibility that I felt as a daughter to be reunited with my family finally won out and I made the decision to leave Germany and immigrate to the United States.

I returned to my hometown of Zschorlau and immediately started to apply for a visa to travel to the western part of Germany where I had to live in order to apply for a visa to the United States. It did not take long for me to find out that to obtain such a permission or visa was totally out of the question. I was denied the request by every agency I approached. After heart-wrenching deliberations and consultations with my Grandfather and my uncles, I decided to travel to Berlin to try my luck there.

At the end of World War II in 1945, the city of Berlin was completely surrounded by territory occupied by Soviet forces. This territory officially became the country of East Germany in 1949. The city of Berlin itself was partitioned into East Berlin and West Berlin. West Berlin was occupied by British, French, and United States forces and was supported by the Federal Republic of Germany, commonly known as West Germany. Many East Germans fled to West Germany hoping to find better economic opportunities there and more than half of them fled through Berlin.

With these facts in mind I had high hopes to be able to find a way to leave East Germany in Berlin with the help of an American Agency in West Berlin. In the year of 1950 travel within Berlin from one sector to another was still permitted and I knew that I would be able to find someone who would help me get across the border into West Germany.

So it came to pass that I left my home and relatives with whom I had grown up with for greener pastures and the land of opportunities. America was so far away and I knew very little about that country, except for an enormous amount of Soviet propaganda that was widely spread to discredit the lifestyle in the West. I had visions of Americans wearing their clothes once, only to throw them away, using disposable plates and cups to avoid having to wash dishes and generally leading a life of capitalistic ideals without putting forth much effort.

Oh, how wrong the propaganda was!

My last few days in Zschorlau were filled with packing and saying" Goodbye" to my relatives and many friends. It was a very emotional time for me, leaving my home without knowing where the path would lead me.

Many tears were shed when the youth group from our Church came to my house the night before my departure to sing a "farewell " song to me. I remember it so well and I must confess that I get teary-eyed still to this day every time I hear this song. In harmony they sang "Gesegnet sei das Band, dass uns im Herrn vereint." In English it is the song "Blest be the tie that binds our hearts in Christian love". It was so meaningful to me and this song will remain special to me for the rest of my life.

It was a day in June of 1950 when I was to board a train at the Bahnhof (train station) in Aue to travel north to Berlin.

My dear old Grandfather had requested to take me to the train-station by himself so we could spend these last precious hours alone together, knowing in our hearts that this would be the last time that we would see each other here on earth. His words that he spoke to me with tears in his eyes will be in my memory forever, and I can still hear him say: "Now is your chance, Anita, to be as free as a bird, take it and fly, and may God watch over you every step of the way." I boarded the very last car on the train so that I would be able to stand on the platform at the end of the train to see my Grandfather as long as I could. It was oh so hard to leave him. We waved to one another as the train left the station and I watched him standing next to the rail road tracks, getting smaller and smaller, until I could see him no more. It was to be the last time that I saw my beloved Grandfather.

Arrangements had been made before I left home that I was to stay with friends of the family in Berlin. The Kamphausen's lived in the western sector of Berlin for which I was very glad, hoping it would help me to obtain a visa for West Germany.

I was very grateful to have a place to stay while I was in Berlin, but as time went on I was becoming more and more uncomfortable in the home of the Kamphausen's. Mrs. Kamphausen was an invalid and was confined to a wheelchair and Mr. Kamphausen was away from home traveling a great deal. A live-in housekeeper was the constant caretaker for Mrs. Kamphausen.

For several weeks after I arrived in Berlin I walked the streets, staring in disbelief at the many ruins and the rubble of beautiful homes, churches and other buildings, still an after effect of the bombings during the war a few short years earlier.

My main objective for being in Berlin was to explore every possibility to obtain a Visa to enter West Germany. All borders were closed for traveling and strict penalties were applied for persons crossing the border illegally. I went to every government agency in West Berlin to apply for a visa and the end result always was a firm "NO." It was extremely frustrating and disappointing to get turned down everywhere I went and I was getting quite desperate. Much talk was circulating about people escaping out of East Germany and Berlin by entering West Germany illegally. It was called going across the border "schwarz" (black).

* * *

During that time I had a letter forwarded to me from my parents who now lived in California with a picture of my little sister Edelgard. She was 13 years old with curly hair and a big smile. It really jolted me into the realization how much I was missing by not being with my own family and, furthermore not knowing my siblings. It made me even more determined to cross the iron curtain and flee into West Germany. I decided to take that tremendously big step and travel west.

Edelgard (Peg) in a 1950 family photo

Kamphausen's did not want me to leave; it had become apparent that they wanted me to stay to become their housekeeper. That was a scary thought and I decided to leave as soon as possible.

* * *

I was in constant contact with my Father's Mission Headquarter in Liebenzell, which wired me the needed money for travel. Two boxes held all of my belongings and I shipped them to Liebenzell. All I had left was my shoulder bag with a few necessary personal items that I carried with me. I exchanged my East German money that I still possessed into West Germany mark and sewed them very carefully into the lining of my coat.

I definitely knew that I was taking a risk, but also felt that risk is the price you pay for opportunity and freedom and I desperately wanted the opportunity to be reunited with my family.

11
Crossing the Border

I was hardly able to sleep the night before my departure from Berlin. I was so excited, but also a bit frightened to enter this new epoch of my life. The long and difficult journey had begun.

It was early in the morning on a cloudy and gray day in the summer of 1950 when I said goodbye to the Kamphausen's and left their home that had been mine for eight weeks, for yet another train-station. I bought a one-way ticket to a city nearest to the border between East and West Germany and traveled by train along the East German countryside until I reached the city of my destination. Unfortunately, I do not remember the name of the city or the name of the village on my itinerary. When I arrived I inquired about a bus that would lead me to a village that was within walking distance to the border. I had to wait several hours for the bus to arrive and almost missed the opportunity for further travel. The bus driver informed me that his only passengers were employees of different companies who worked in the city but lived in the nearby village. I was crushed and asked him to please make an exception and take me along. With his right thumb he pointed in the direction toward the west and asked me if I intended to cross the border. I answered him with an emphatic "yes" and he let me enter his bus.

I was so happy to be on my way.

The bus we were traveling in was a very old fashioned and dilapidated, rough riding vehicle, but it did not matter to me, as it would take me to the road to freedom.

After we had traveled for some time, several Soviet Border Police who were controlling the area stopped the bus. The bus and its passengers were to be checked for valid passports. During these post war years every citizen in East Germany was obligated to carry a current pass-board and or identification papers with them at all times. Every person was registered at police headquarters and it was mandatory to report the departure of the town one was registered in and register again in the city or town that was to be visited over night or longer.

So it was not unusual that the bus I was on would have a "Razzia," a police raid.

Unfortunately, my identification was not valid in the area that I was traveling in and thus I experienced my first "close encounter."

The seats of the bus were open underneath and were placed facing each other. Several older men were sitting beside and across from me who turned out to be my guardian angels. When it became apparent that our bus was going to be stopped and inspected, I was quite frightened and my face must have given away my fear. One of the men said to me "Hide under the seat and we will cover you up with our coats." My heart was pounding as I crawled under the seat and awaited my fate. I heard the doors of the bus open up and the Russian Patrol guard entered to proceed with his inspection of pass boards. I trusted God who had brought me this far to protect me from the "enemy patrol." As I hovered there, I watched the big boots of the policeman walk to the back of the bus, stopping at every seat to inspect the identification of the passengers and as he passed my seat I was sure that he would hear the pounding of my heart. But he passed my row of seats without noticing me hiding under one of them. After several minutes the boots that I had seen walking toward the back of the bus earlier were now walking past me in the opposite direction toward the front of the bus. Soon the guard exited and we were on our way. I slowly came out of my hiding place and sat back in my seat amidst my newly made friends and protectors. I was so grateful to these wonderful men!

The wheels of the old bus rolled on toward the border that divided Germany.

There was only one stop in the middle of the small village that was the destination of the bus trip. Everyone left the bus and in order not to look suspicious to anyone who might be watching me, I zeroed in on a house that was in my vision and walked toward it. Not knowing who and what I might find in that strange house, I knocked on the door... A lady answered the door looking at me with a questioning expression, suspicion in her eyes, perhaps. I am sure that she saw a helpless creature in front of her asking and begging for help. "Do you know of anyone who can show me the way across the border" I asked her? What a chance I took in confessing what I had in mind doing. What if the lady was a communist, a spy, and a sympathizer of the enemy or a German idealist? LORD, HELP ME, I silently prayed.

"I have a grandson and a granddaughter who show people, such as you, where to cross the border and help them along the way," she said. "However, you will have to pay a good sum of money to compensate them for the risk they are taking."

"I will give them all of my East German money that I have," was my reply, and that was agreeable. The young teens were summoned and I was told that the time to start our venture would be immediately, for the time was right for the border guards to change their shifts. While they were busy exchanging their daily reports, our chances of not being noticed easily were quite good.

So the venture to cross the border between East and West Germany, illegally, had begun!

The small convoy consisted of the teenage boy with his bicycle, his sister who was also a teen and myself who actually was a teenager as well. I carried a small bag, not much larger than a big handbag that held my most needed possessions.

My young friend with the bicycle instructed us to follow his lead. He would ride along the road while we were to hide behind a bush, in a ditch bank, behind a tree or any other cover we could find. As soon as he got off his bike, we were to walk quickly until we saw him getting on his bike again. We followed that same procedure for quite some time. At his last stop we caught up with him and he told me that this was as far as he and his sister would accompany me. He pointed to a farmhouse in the near distance and told me that once I reached that destination I had crossed the border. The two teens left me to return to their village as soon as I had given them all the East German money I possessed, as I had promised.

I can still remember how I felt when I stood at a crossroad in this German countryside, exhilarated and thrilled to have made it thus far, but mostly I felt as free as a bird to have escaped the Russian government and the communist regime that was so frightening and confining to me. I was one step further towards meeting my family in the USA. Standing at this crossroad, which was actually an area that was called "No Man's Land," I was very uncertain which road to take to continue my journey.

I made a decision and as I started walking along this country road I encountered another obstacle. Two West German border policemen on horseback came riding toward me, they looked rather intimidating but I tried hard not to let it show.

"Well, young Lady, where do you come from? And where do you think you are going?" the one officer said to me. I replied," I come directly from Berlin and am on my way to the next town or city."

"Berlin," he said, "that is my hometown and I have not been back since the war ended. What does the City look like and what are the general conditions there?" he asked. Here was my chance to distract him and in a few minutes I told him everything I had ever heard or seen in Berlin. He was very attentive, but soon interrupted me and informed me that it really was their duty as border police officers to send me back to where I came from. I pleaded with both of them to please let me continue my journey and told them my story of wanting to be reunited with my family in the US. A miracle happened. They let me go! Not only did they let me go free, they directed me where to go next. The Officer from Berlin wrote a little note instructing me to walk along the road we were on until I came to a Border Patrol station. On the note it said that he gave me permission to stay at the station until the daily postal truck arrived which would take me along to the next city. I could not believe my good fortune and again prayed a prayer of thanksgiving. When I arrived at the little Patrol station I was welcomed with something to drink and fortunately there was time for me to clean myself up a bit and to undo the lining of my coat to retrieve my West German money that I had hidden in the lining of my coat. I was truly exhausted by that time and the ride in the postal truck, amidst bundles of letters and packages, was such a welcome relief.

It was late when we arrived at the city of Wolfburg where my personal chauffeur of the postal truck took me directly to the train station. I immediately sent a telegram to my Grandfather telling him that I was safe, and I am sure that he felt greatly relieved. I was 18 years old when I crossed the border between East and West Germany.

I had enough money to purchase a train ticket for Bad Liebenzell, the Mission Headquarters of my parents. It was the Liebenzell Mission that financed my journey for which I was so grateful. The train was not due to arrive for another hour and it was the middle of the night by then. Few people were in sight and it was rather dark in the train station. To get to the platform where trains arrive and depart I had to walk down a flight of stairs, walk through a tunnel-like walkway and up the stairs to reach the platform where I would get on the train. As I was walking along, I heard footsteps behind me and the faster I walked, the faster the footsteps became. I was terrified as my pursuer caught up with me asking me, or rather telling me to come with him to his place. As I was arguing with him, trying to free myself of him I saw a little control station on the platform near the stairs. I ran toward it and saw several men who controlled the train switches in the little glass

Control Station. It displayed a sign saying: "Eintritt verboten," which means entrance forbidden, but I ignored the sign and pounded on the glass door, which was locked, until someone opened it. I asked for help and was allowed to stay with the train officials until my train arrived.

I did not see the man who pursued me again.

The train was nearly empty and as I sat on the hard bench on that dark train it finally sank in what I had done and in what grave danger I had placed myself.

I felt so alone...

It was then that I really became frightened and it was then that I knew that God Himself led me across the border and was with me every step of this dangerous journey. My tears were a combination of relief and gratitude...

I arrived in Bad Liebenzell the next morning where I was warmly welcomed, bathed and fed. Several friends of my parents still lived there in the Mission Home and I felt very safe and secure.

My sister Eva lived in Tuttlingen where she was just finishing her nurse's training. She was called immediately after my arrival and a date was made when I was to meet her in Tuttlingen at the Hospital where she was in training and also lived as a student nurse. The Regional Hospital in Tuttlingen was staffed and run by the Liebenzell Mission and most of the nurses were Liebenzell Sisters.

12

Tuttlingen, 1950 - 1953

It was wonderful to see my sister Eva again. I called her Evchen, as most of our family members did, and it felt good to have someone as close as a sister to lean on.

I got a job at the Hospital in the Diet Department of the Kitchen and since I had been trained in that area it was natural for me to work there. I soon became well acquainted with all the functions of my job and worked well with the staff. I filled in for the main Dietician, as well as the manager of the whole department, and enjoyed what I was doing.

Eva and I lived away from the hospital and each had a small room in a near by one family dwelling. The rooms were very small and consisted of a bed, a small dresser and a wardrobe for our clothes. There were no frills, no radio, desk or cooking facilities. It was strictly a room for sleeping. We both worked long hours at the hospital and also ate all of our meals there. There was no place were we could entertain friends or family, so Eva and I went out a lot on our free time.

On Sunday afternoons we often went to a coffee house that was called "Café Schlack" for our entertainment. There was always an orchestra playing that we enjoyed listening to while we had our afternoon coffee and pastry. Café Schlack was a very popular place for young people and it didn't take us long to make friends.

Eva and I both went out on dates often, to go dancing or to a movie and enjoyed ourselves with what life had to offer us.

* * *

The responsibility of my job was often difficult for me and quite overwhelming for an 18 -20 year old. I remember one incident that I had to cope with that was very hard on me. I was in charge of the whole kitchen department for one week while the lady who normally held that position was on vacation, when I caught our key employee stealing meat from the big walk-in refrigerator. As I was talking to her she confessed that she had been stealing from the Hospital Kitchen for quite some time. I was devastated to have to fire her; she was close to retirement and had been a very good employee. My employer backed me up and reassured me that I had made the right decision.

Very soon after I arrived in Tuttlingen we started working on getting our Visas to travel to the United

States. The first stage was handled in Stuttgart and later we had to go to Muenchen to the American Consulate. We had so hoped that we could soon be on our way to America to meet our family, but it seemed that one obstacle after another arose that kept us from getting our Visa. One reason was the fact that we were both in the Hitler Youth in earlier years, which was absurd, since we had no choice in the matter. Another reason, perhaps the biggest obstacle, was the fact that we were both born in China and had to come on a Chinese quota. They were very rare and hard to come by. So we waited while the red tape continued to roll and the officials hashed out our future.

* * *

In the meantime our parents, as well as our sister Esther, brother Fred and sister Edelgard moved from California to Scottsbluff, Nebraska, where Papa was asked to minister in the Zion Evangelical Lutheran Church. The members of the congregation were of Russian-German descent and many of them were not proficient in the English language and needed a pastor who was able to preach in the German as well as the English Language. Of course Papa qualified and thus he became their Pastor. My brother Hans stayed in California to attend UCLA.

My father often corresponded with the American Consulate in regard to our Immigration Visas and their status and became very impatient with the unreasonable length of time it took for their completion. In late 1952 he decided to take matters into his own hands and contacted the Representative of Nebraska A.L. Miller, employing him to check into the matter. Very shortly thereafter Eva and I were notified that our Visas were ready to be signed and sealed in Muenchen.

While we lived in Tuttlingen, we made frequent trips to Offenburg in Baden, the hometown of our Mother, to visit her two sisters with their families who still lived there. We loved visiting Tante Elise; she was trying so hard to take the place of our Mother while we were with them and pampered us a great deal. Tante Didi was widowed; her daughter Gretel was still living with her, taking care of her mother who was an invalid. I was happy to meet the sisters of my mother and often imagined that Tante Elise was much like my mother, very sweet and gentle.

It was while we were in Offenburg on one of our weekend trips visiting our relatives that we were notified that our trip to the United States was scheduled and that we were to leave on the 12th of March, 1953.

It was with bittersweet emotions that Eva and I started to pack our bags and thought about leaving Tuttlingen. I had been dating a young man with whom I was madly in love and the thought of leaving him broke my heart. His name was Hubert Bender. Of course we promised each other eternal love, as young lovers do, but there would be an ocean between us....

* * *

Eva had become engaged to Johannes Grohmann and was devastated about saying her goodbyes to him, not knowing when she would see him again.

* * *

My Father, Max Wilhelm, in WWI

My Mother's Grandmother (Maria Cron, the adult in the photo) and Mother (top right) in front of Castle Stolzenfels

My Mother (center) as a deaconess with her two sisters

Young missionary Wilhelm (left) with friends

Max and Anna Wilhelm, married September 2, 1927 in Hungkiang.

Max & Anna Wilhelm, approximately 1926

My 2nd Birthday

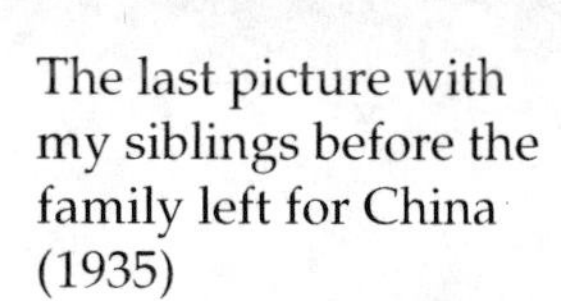

The last picture with my siblings before the family left for China (1935)

My family at their Summer home in China, named after me.

My Grandmother Ida Wilhelm (right) with her Mother, Anna Doerfelt

My Grandfather who raised me, Oskar Wilhelm

My childhood home

First day of school

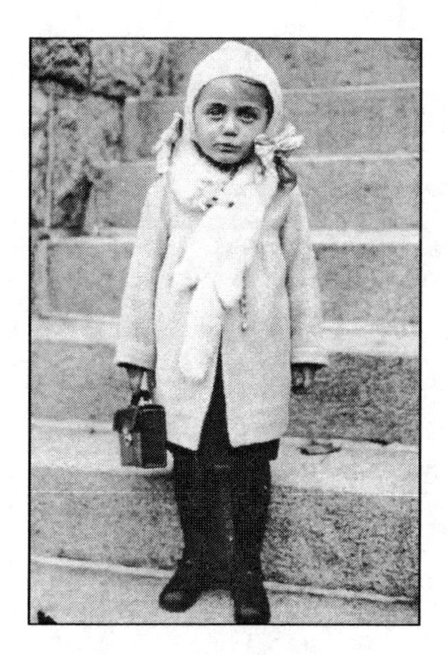

5 years old with a fur…

Let's go sledding!

After a passport photo session, my Grandfather's photographer suggested a quick shot with me – one of my favorite pictures of my "Vater."

First visit with sister Eva upon her arrival from China in 1941

With sister Eva at her confirmation

My confirmation with my cousin and best friend, Inge

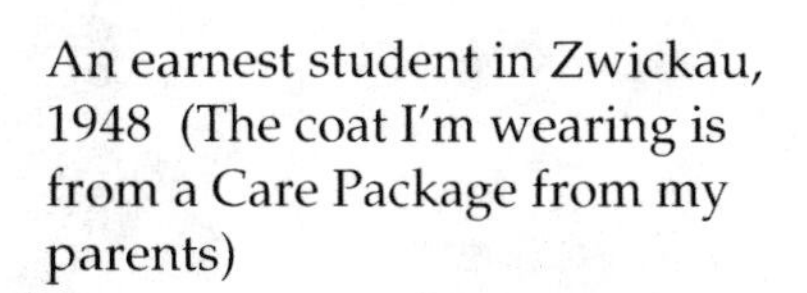

An earnest student in Zwickau, 1948 (The coat I'm wearing is from a Care Package from my parents)

The last photo of me before leaving Germany (in Offenburg)

The SS United States

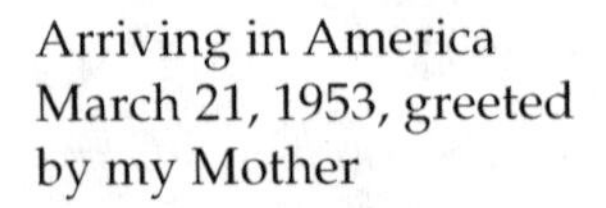

Arriving in America March 21, 1953, greeted by my Mother

English class with Mrs. Hannibal - Sprechen Sie Englisch?

Two single girls in America (sister Eva & me)

My Cowboy Bill

William Dale Osborn, no longer an eligible bachelor

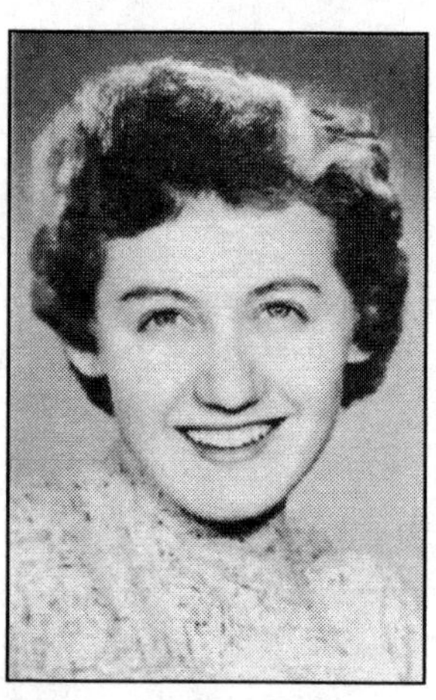

My engagement photo, with lots to smile about!

December 31, 1955 – our big day!

My Parents,
Max and Anna Wilhelm

Bill's Parents,
Caroline and Art Osborn

First one…

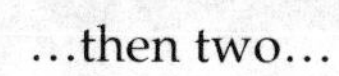

…then two…

…then all three!

Stevie on the road...

...and at birthday parties

Donny in the portrait studio...

...and on the street

Jenny with her Grandad...

...and at school

Our first and last complete family reunion (standing l-r) Esther, Me, Hans, Fred, Peggy (seated) Mutti, Eva and Papa

Esther upon graduation from Nursing School

Esther and Don Klett with their children (l-r) Laurie, Karla and Donna). This is Esther's last picture, taken in January of 1967. She died later that month.

From kids to teenagers…

...to parents, with families of their own

Jenny and Pat Bashford with their children
(l-r) David, Sarah and Andy

Steve and Barb Osborn
with their children (l-r)
Becky, Neil and Annie

Don Osborn with his son, Tyler

Bill and I in the late 70s...

...and today

13
Coming to America

After we had said our goodbyes in Tuttlingen and our luggage was taken care of, we went to Offenburg from where we would take the train to Bremerhafen. Aunt Elise and Uncle Karl accompanied us on this last trek in Germany.

A special train took us to the Columbus Wharf and from there we boarded our ship, the S.S. United States. It was at that time the largest and most luxurious ship ever built in America and the world's fastest and most modern Liner. We felt very fortunate to be able to sail on this beautiful ocean liner, which would take us to the "land of honey and unlimited opportunities."

The ship seemed to us like a big floating hotel as we tried to find our way to our staterooms. They seemed very beautiful to us and we were very excited in a special kind of way. There were bands playing "Auf Wiedersehen, Auf Wiedersehen" as we stood on deck at the railing looking back at the many people who were well-wishers and friends and family of the passengers. Many people on both sides cried and waved their handkerchiefs to say their final good byes. Finally, the ship left the harbor and the city with its buildings became smaller and smaller.

My feelings were mixed. I was very sad to leave my home country where I had lived all of my life, but excited and thrilled to be one step closer to meeting my family.

I conveyed some of my feeling in a letter to my Aunt and Uncle Richter just before we left for Bremerhaven, telling them how frightened I was of what was ahead of me and what might happen to me in this strange country with it's strange language, customs and a new culture. Most of all I was concerned about meeting my parents at age 21, as well as my siblings. What if we did not bond, or understand each other in a way that I wished for. Realizing that it must be very difficult for my parents too to meet an adult daughter that was a stranger to them. So many frightening thoughts and "what ifs" entered my mind!

In the beginning of our voyage we could hardly feel the ship moving, it was very pleasant and we enjoyed sailing.

The first time the ship stopped was in Le Havre, and the second time in South Hampton, where another one thousand passengers embarked. After we left South Hampton, the sea became very rough and I, among many of the Passengers, succumbed to seasickness. I must say that seasickness is the most horrible illness one can have. I missed many meals and stayed in our cabin day after day. According to my sister, there was a lot offered to entertain the ship's guests, but many of us were not interested, nor were we able to take advantage of the hours of fun. Later in the week I felt somewhat better and went into the dining room for dinner with my sister. The food was plentiful, but quite strange to us and we often did not know what to order. I remember one time when the steward came to our table asking for our preference from the menu, Eva said "Oh, just bring us everything." What she meant to say was bring us anything. Her statement brought some giggles from a neighboring table and a gentleman who overheard the conversation offered to help us order from then on. Most of the stewards were black, something we were not accustomed to, but they were very friendly and helpful. After dinner many passengers went to play "Bingo," something we had never heard of and didn't quite understand. Instead of playing Bingo we went to the ballroom and listened to a band play popular music. One night the band's lead singer sang "Bay Mir Bistu Sheyn" which was a popular song in the States at the time, but we were so incensed with the wrong pronunciation that we left the ballroom.

Our voyage from Bremerhaven to New York took six days in all and March 19th was the target day of our arrival in New York. We knew that our Mother had come to New York from Nebraska to be the first member of the family to greet her two daughters, whom she had not seen for so many years.

So many passengers stood on deck eager to see the first strip of land, the land that was called America. The land of opportunities and freedom! Slowly, the skyline of New York became distinguishable and it was so exciting to see the many skyscrapers that I had seen in movies and had read about. What an incredible sight.

We were to anchor at eight AM but had to wait four more long hours before the United States was able to sail into the harbor of the Hudson Bay.

Eva and I, along with many others, stood on deck overlooking the pier and the masses of people awaiting passengers from the ship. Our mother was among them, but where was she and what did she look like? We scanned the crowd looking and looking for her. As different ladies came into view that might fit our mother's description, I would ask Eva, "Do you think this is Mutti?" but her reply was always, "No, I don't think so." All of a sudden we heard someone call Eva's name, it was an old friend who was in school with her in China and had come to the States earlier. She was kind enough to escort our Mother to the ship and had spotted us. At that moment we saw a lady and knew instantly that it was our Mother, as she knew that we were her daughters. What a feeling that was...

Three hours later we were finally allowed to walk down the gangplank to go on land. Several bands were playing and it was a very festive atmosphere when we finally found our mother. So many tears of joy and laughter were shed and it was such a happy occasion, one that I had dreamed of for so many years.

Our first stop on our way to Nebraska was in Schooley's Mountain in New Jersey, the American Branch of the Liebenzell Mission. We were there for only a short time when we resumed our travel by train on to Philadelphia to visit friends of my parents who had also been missionaries in China. The first days after we arrived in New York seem to be a blur to me and I don't remember any details. We were so tired from travel, the time change, and of course all the newness that came upon us.

From Philadelphia we traveled on to Chicago and arrived nineteen hours later. It was there that I met my sister Esther for the first time. She was in nursing school in one of the hospitals in Chicago. We stayed with the Kamphausens who were German missionaries who had been with my parents in China and were close friends. Missionary Kamphausen was the brother of Mr. Kamphausen with whom I stayed in Berlin. Esther came to see us every day while we were there and I really felt that we bonded quickly, she was such a sweet and wonderful girl and I was so thrilled to finally meet her.

Soon, the last leg of our trip began. Again we boarded a train heading for Nebraska. Our final destination was Gering, Nebraska, the twin city of Scottsbluff. The train trip was twenty-two hours long and seemed unending.

We sat, slept and ate on the train that took us through the vastness of America. We had no idea just how big this country was and couldn't believe that it could take so many hours to travel within one country. In Germany we could travel anywhere within a few hours and the trains were a lot more comfortable. Our train had no sleeping cars, and we slept on our seats that were upholstered and cushiony, which made the trip more bearable.

The American food was very foreign to us and it took some time to get accustomed to it. I remember getting some popcorn on the train. Mutti thought it would be a treat for us, but Eva and I didn't like it at all; it tasted so dry and flavorless.

The train's wheels rumbled on and on over the long stretches of Nebraska's prairie and it seemed endless until we finally arrived in Gering. The long train ride gave me lots of time to think about the new epoch of my life that was about to begin. I had very mixed emotions and have to admit was a little frightened of what lay ahead of me. Trust and faith were the words that came to mind over and over again and knowing that God had brought me this far, I believed that He would continue to guide me through this period of my life.

We arrived in Gering, Nebraska and Papa, Fred and Nucki, which was a family nickname for my sister Edelgard, later known as Peggie, were at the train-station to welcome us. What a long awaited moment that was! After so many days of traveling by ship and trains, it was a real relief to finally be at "Home." We had a very joyful reunion in Scottsbluff, Nebraska, a small town in the middle of America that was to be our new home. By the time I finally arrived in Scottsbluff, I had been separated from my parents for 18 years.

Our new address was 1423 8th Avenue. Our family home was the Parsonage of the Zion Evangelical Lutheran Church in Scottsbluff, of which Papa was the pastor. The congregation of the church consisted mainly of Russian-German people who for the most part were farmers in the surrounding area. Their history is very interesting and colorful dating back to the years of the 1740's when a German Princess married the Russian Emperor Peter the Third. After his murder, Katherine was crowned empress and hence was called Katherine II, the Great.

Katherine was the first to begin planned settlement of agricultural colonists in the uncultivated areas in the south of Russia. Most of the colonists came from Germany. The main reasons for so many Germans to immigrate to Russia at Katherine's beckoning were the following: economic, political, and religious. At that time, for part of the population, emigration seemed the only way out.

Life in Russia was hard for the Germans, but they guarded their German traditions throughout the generations, maintaining the customs and dialects of their ancestral homeland.

At the end of the 1800s the Czar revoked many rights and privileges that had been offered to the

Germans by Katherine the Great. As a result, they were reduced to the level of the Russian peasants and their sons were drafted into the Czar's army. These conditions created much unrest and dissatisfaction among the German settlers and brought about the movement for emigration to the United States.

Many of the emigrants settled in Colorado, the Dakotas and in our North Platte Valley in Western Nebraska.

* * *

The house on 8th Avenue was a simple wood structure with a finished basement and had plenty of room for the whole family. A nice yard of grass and flowers, shrubs and trees surrounded our home. The flowers were Mutti's pride and joy, but it was Papa's job to water the lawn. It might have been a simple home by American standards, but for Eva and me it was a wonderful big house with so many comforts that we had not known before. We were intrigued with the central heating system, a large kitchen with an electric stove, washing machine and wall-to-wall carpet, and of course a telephone right in the house; that was luxury.

I shared a bedroom with my sister Peggie, and we often talked long into the night about all the things that we had missed out on in earlier years.

Peggie was a sixteen-year-old teenager, full of life and lots of fun. She taught me many of the American customs and eating habits that were new to me. We soon bonded... Eva had a bedroom next to ours and my brother Fred lived in the basement of the home. He was the first person that I saw wearing "cowboy boots and a big cowboy hat." Fred was a senior in high school when we arrived and graduated that spring. Shortly after I met him, he gave me a gold ring with a Chinese insignia. The ring, which he had brought from China, was his prized possession; I was very touched by that loving gesture.

* * *

Scottsbluff, Nebraska is situated about 20 miles from the Wyoming state line and almost centered in the panhandle of Nebraska. The town is located on the north side of the North Platte River and was named after a fur trapper, Hiram Scott, who was traveling through the area. History reports that he and his friends were in a skirmish with some Indians when Hiram Scott was wounded. His friends knew that he could not survive the long trip to St. Louis under these difficult conditions and left him behind. As the story goes, he managed to find a spring close to the base of the bluffs. There he died, and his remains were found at a later date near a bluff, which was named Scott's Bluff in his memory. As a result, the nearby town was called Scottsbluff.

The famous Oregon Trail was located on the south side of the river and the Mormon trail came through on the north side of the river. There are several noteworthy landmarks in the area going back to the days of fur-traders and wagon trains. They are Chimney Rock, Courthouse Rock and Jailhouse Rock, Mitchell Pass and Robidoux Pass, to name a few. The whole area is semi-arid, and I have to admit that I missed the trees that were in such abundance in my homeland of Germany. However, the picturesque town of Scottsbluff that was so typically American, as well as the sleepy little towns in the whole county, made up for the missing trees and forests.

In general, I found living in Scottsbluff very comfortable and I liked it. I was intrigued with the "laid back" style of living that was so customary in this farming community and the friendly and generous people surrounding me. I believe that my expectations far exceeded my wildest dreams and I can say that I never regretted my decision of coming to the United States.

Coming from post-war Germany where destruction, rubble and ashes from the Second World War were still very evident and many of the comforts that Americans take for granted were still unthinkable and unavailable, made this place seem like a land of milk and honey.

As one can well imagine, many adjustments had to be made with moving to a new country. One of the biggest obstacles for me was the fact that I did not speak English. I had had all of my education in the eastern block of Germany, which was occupied and governed by the Communist Russian Regime; it banned all English language classes and replaced them with Russian language classes. Consequently, I only spoke German when I arrived in the United States. The every day language spoken in our home was German; therefore, I had to find other sources of learning the English language.

Eva and I enrolled in an evening course at the local college and at the same time decided we needed to find jobs to bring us into the main stream of life here in

America. We had only been in the States for a few weeks when we started working.

Eva was a nurse and was able to find employment at the Methodist Hospital in Scottsbluff in her profession. I got a job at the Hospital Food Service and since I had been a dietician in Germany I felt that I would be able to do my job without vocalizing a great deal. I was very fortunate in that several Russian-German ladies worked at the diet department with me and I could communicate with them. They were very helpful to me and I was very grateful to these German ladies for assisting me whenever I needed help

Our night classes at the college progressed nicely and it didn't take us too long before we were able to communicate in English fairly well. I remember sitting on the front porch steps at the parsonage with my sister Peggie and her friend Liz Banghart, who lived across the street, as they tried to help me with the pronunciation of a number of words with which I had difficulty. I especially remember the words "Brussels Sprouts, Potatoes and Tomatoes" that gave me problems.

Living with my family was often not easy and caused me much heartache at times. Having lived on my own for many years and being totally responsible for myself made it very difficult to adhere to Papa's strict measures of discipline. China was home for my parents for almost three decades; moving to America caused them to experience a total culture shock. It definitely showed in the way they treated their grown-up children. We were not allowed to go to movies, go dancing or heaven forbid, go out with young men; in other words, go out on dates. My father's opinion was that as the children of a pastor we had to set a good example to the young people in his congregation. We were expected to go to all church services, as well as belong to the youth group that met on Sunday nights. When we were asked to sing in the church choir I was very thrilled because I had sung in church choirs, as well as other choirs in Germany, and always loved music and looked forward to sing in a choir again. Eva and I were often asked to sing duets together and we enjoyed that because we were able to choose our own music. We liked singing in German, which was requested by many church members when we sang for funerals, weddings or other church functions.

We met other young people who belonged to the church youth group. After meetings on Sunday night, we usually went out as a group to a local drive-in to have a coke and french fries. I remember one time when we arrived home after ten o'clock we really got into trouble. Papa was absolutely furious with us and called us all sorts of names. As punishment for our sinful deed we had to do the family laundry the next day. We were disgusted and frustrated, and Eva and I were ready to move into a place of our own. But unfortunately, we did not have any funds for a move because Papa handled our money. We had to turn in our paychecks as soon as we received them and had to ask for spending money. Our father monitored every penny we spent. Of course the money was saved for us, but we did not have an opportunity to handle our own finances or make any purchases on our own.

My biggest heartache was that I was forbidden to have any contact with my boyfriend Hubert Bender in Germany. When my father learned that Hubert's religious affiliation was Catholic he literally told me to stop any communication with him. I was heart-broken... I received letters from Hubert for a while via the hospital address I had given him, but was always frightened that Papa would find out about my deceit. Hubert and I finally decided that we had no future together and broke up.

I remember sharing my "love letters" with my little sister while we were sitting on our bed, both of us sobbing. It was a very difficult time for me to accept Papa's harsh commands. But life went on...

As I look back I realize that Papa had our best interests and our well being in mind, and that he loved us. However, his way was often difficult to understand.

After I had been working at the diet department in the hospital for a few months, Max Coppom, the hospital's administrator, approached me one day and asked me if I would not rather work in the hospital's front office, than in the kitchen. My reply was that I was not sure if I was sufficiently proficient in English to work in the office. He assured me, however, that it was, and asked me to give it a try. I was thrilled with the confidence he showed in me and agreed to take on the challenge.

To my surprise, I was assigned to the main telephone switchboard. All incoming and outgoing telephone calls filtered through the switchboard and I was responsible to answer them all. There must have been fifty telephone jacks on the big switchboard, and at times it seemed they were all ringing at once. It was a wonderful way to get acquainted with the hospital personnel, as well as all of the doctors and technicians. I liked my new position very well and worked several different shifts, as well as on Sundays when it was my turn.

* * *

The summer of 1953 was unseasonably hot and we often went on an outing to Lake Minatare to go swimming and to get cooled off from the heat in town. Air-conditioning was non-existent at that time. Lake Minatare is a man-made lake about 14 miles north east of Scottsbluff and its main purpose is to supply water for irrigation to the farmland in the Valley.

It became a great recreational area for camping, fishing, boating and swimming, as well as a much sought after place for picnics.

* * *

It was during that time in the summer that I meet Jeanne Brown. Jeanne worked with me at the hospital office, and we ultimately became lifelong friends.

Jeanne lived on a farm in Mitchell Valley and she invited me often to her home to spend the night. She was a typical American "next door" kind of girl, so easy to be with. We understood each other perfectly. Her parents, Dorothy and Ken, were very kind to me and I felt very comfortable and at ease with them. I often had a date while I was staying at Jeanne's house, and thus bypassing Papa's rules about dating. None of the dates I had were of a serious nature, but it was fun to go to a movie or out to dinner with a young man. Jeanne and I often spent time at my house as well. Mutti and Papa were very fond of her and encouraged our relationship.

I remember so well the first time Hans came to visit from Los Angeles, California where he attended U.C.L.A. He arrived in Cheyenne and the whole family went to meet him at the station. I was so excited to meet my older brother whom I had not seen since I was a three- year- old little girl.

He was a good looking young man, very friendly and outgoing, and I ached to get to know him. For some reason I was very shy and it was hard for me to communicate easily with Hans. I envied Eva, who was very close to him and was able to talk with him so freely. I deeply regretted not having grown up with my siblings and felt lonely and left out while in their midst. My insecurity about not having bonded with my family in my formative years became very apparent. I often felt so homesick even though I was home. It was all so confusing to me and my emotions ran hot and cold.

My sister Esther, who lived in Chicago, also came to visit once or twice during the first year that I lived in

Scottsbluff. I began to feel very close to Esther and felt that a sisterly bond was developing between us. I was very grateful for that gift. Papa and Mutti tried so hard to have all of us six children together at one time, but it never worked out. The times when Hans was able to come from California, it was not possible for Esther to get away from her nurses training and therefore we were never together under one roof for years to come.

In the winter of 1954, I was approached by the Community College to teach evening classes in "Conversational German" at the Adult Education Department. It was a wonderful opportunity for me to teach German to adults who wanted to further their skills in the German language and to help them to learn not only the language, but also introduce them to the customs and traditions of the German culture. Many of my students had plans to travel abroad and were grateful to be able to learn some very practical and useful phrases in German. Two of my students were American teachers who were assigned to live in Germany for a few years to teach the children of military families who were stationed there.

At the end of each semester there was a social function for the class and each student brought their spouse or a friend. Peggy Alberts, who was one of the teachers leaving for Germany brought a young man she was dating to the party. His name was Bill Osborn. Bill was to become my husband.

* * *

In early 1955, Eva's fiancé, Johannes Grohmann, was informed that his visa application to come to the United States was denied and he was not able to immigrate to America to marry Eva. It was a terrible shock to her and to the whole family, as we had all planned on Eva and Johannes living here with us in the States. It was hard for Mutti and Papa to give up their oldest daughter again, but she had no choice but to return to Germany to get married and to live there. She was very disappointed, but eager to get back together with her intended. How plans change in a lifetime.

* * *

The plan was for Mutti and Papa to drive Eva to New York to board the ship, stopping in Chicago to pick up Esther who was joining them on this long drive to New York. Before they left, Mutti made a beautiful wedding dress for Eva, but we were sad that none of us would be able to see her as a bride in Germany and witness her wedding. When the last trunk and suitcase was packed, Mutti, Papa and Eva began their trip to New York, via Chicago.

* * *

While driving on the Pennsylvania Turnpike during a hurricane, Papa had a terrible automobile accident, leaving Mutti seriously injured. She was hospitalized and Esther stayed with her while Papa took Eva to the pier in New York. It was a difficult time for all of us, especially Eva, who had to say good-bye to Mutti and Papa under these sad circumstances.

My sister Peggie had graduated from High School in May of 1955 and attended an airline school in Omaha, Nebraska. Fred had graduated two years earlier and had enlisted in the United States Air Force. Peggie came home while our parents were on their lengthy trip to New York, and we kept each other company.

* * *

It was during that time that I had my first date with Bill Osborn.

I had actually met him again after our initial meeting at my German class social gathering. Our church youth group and Bill's youth group from his church, The United Methodist Church, had a combined party earlier in the year. It was held at his father's place of business, The Tent and Awning Company, a big building that was close to his house. Eva was still here and we went together with other youth from our church. We all had a really good time and I was hoping to see Bill again some time soon, even though he didn't pay too much attention to me at the party.

During the following months we saw each other occasionally and on the 11th of August we had our first date. We went to a popular place for dinner called "The Stable Club" and had a wonderful time. He called me every day and we went out almost every night. This was during the time when my parents were away and I was very concerned about what I would do when they returned home, knowing how my father felt about the subject of dating. It worried me a great deal, but I had such a good time with Bill that I put any concerns I had out of my mind.

Mutti was pretty badly injured and was still in bad shape when Papa brought her home. My heart ached for both of them. Mutti had several facial cuts and her nose had been broken and she was still in a lot of pain. Papa felt very badly for having been responsible for the accident, causing her such misery.

Shortly after our parents returned, Peggie left home to begin her job in Washington, D.C. It was quite an undertaking for an eighteen year old to accept a job so far away from home, but she was courageous and full of hope and expectations for a wonderful new life in the nations capitol. I would miss her a lot. It left me alone at home now with my parents, but I had high hopes to be able to establish a good and meaningful relationship with them.

* * *

Papa was very highly respected and liked by his congregation, as well as his friends from the Ministerial Association in the whole area. His preaching was very straightforward, directly from the bible and always delivered with a passion for bringing souls to the Lord. I admired him and loved him dearly, and regretted that I had never known him as a child to be held on his knee, or taken by the hand to guide me across the street. Oh, so many things happen between a father and his child that I missed out on. Consequently, I did not feel at ease with my father one on one and it was not easy for me to communicate with him. The Bond was missing, no matter how hard I tried. Often, I felt that I did not measure up to his expectations.

Mutti was a wonderful woman, kind and gentle with a sweet spirit. She was much loved by everyone. I treasured spending time with her and we had a lot in common. We often marveled when we discovered how similarly we approached certain tasks, especially in the kitchen, considering the fact that I didn't learn any habits from her while I was young,

She was an excellent cook and a good homemaker, and had a gift of making any guests feel welcome and comfortable in her home. I was introduced to Chinese food and learned to love it, as my family did. Papa said that one had to eat Chinese food with chopsticks for it to taste good, so I learned to do that and I had to agree with Papa on that subject.

Mutti loved her children unconditionally, and I learned from my siblings how much fun she was when she was young and how creative she became on holidays with very limited resources in the primitive country of China. I can only imagine and wonder what it must have been like...

* * *

My mother was a very faithful wife and never spoke out against anything Papa said or did. I hardly ever heard her complain about anything; she lived the life of a true Christian. My parents were very committed to each other and had a special relationship, serving the Lord wherever they were asked to minister.

14
William Dale Osborn

The first time Bill invited me out after my parents had returned from the East Coast, I asked him to meet me in front of Hausermann's Drugstore in downtown Scottsbluff. I received a very firm reply. He said; "I will pick you up at your home and return you there after our date." It took me almost a whole week to find the courage to tell Papa about my date. He was not very happy about it, because he had not met Bill, and was less than friendly to him when he picked me up. It became easier for me once I told Papa that I was going to date Bill. That fall Papa had to go to a church conference out of town and left Mutti in my care. Since I didn't want to leave her alone at home at night, Bill came to our home, instead of our going out. We spent several evenings together with Mutti, popping popcorn, having snacks and coffee, and enjoying a good time together. I was so glad that Mutti was able to get acquainted with my boyfriend and she liked him from the start.

Bill was a very caring, friendly, considerate and loving young man who was easy to like and so comfortable to be with. He was the most wonderful man I had ever met and, without a doubt, I was beginning to fall in love with him. Bill was of medium height with curly reddish blond hair and was very good looking. I often stole glances at his profile while we were driving in his car, and I was so happy to be with him whenever we were together. It soon became very apparent to me that I wanted to spend the rest of my life with Bill. I felt like I had finally come home.

One Saturday night, the 30th of September, Bill took me to the "Copper Kettle" for dinner. After we dined, he gave me the best gift a young woman could receive... a beautiful diamond ring. He lovingly put the ring on my finger and asked me to be his wife. The ring bound our hearts together and like a band of iron forged our lives to each other. I was so certain that Bill was the right man for me to marry and to be my partner for life that I said yes to him without hesitating. We made a commitment to each other that was the beginning of our life together.

Bill made a trip to the parsonage to ask Papa officially for my hand. Not knowing Bill, or his family, Papa was quite apprehensive and somewhat concerned for my well-being. Perhaps he was disappointed that he was not consulted before we made our commitment to each other. He was somewhat non-committal, but accepted our decision to get married. Bill was twenty-five years old and I was two years younger.

William Dale Osborn was born on January 7, 1930, in Scottsbluff, Nebraska, the son of Arthur and Caroline Osborn. He grew up and received his education in Scottsbluff, graduating from high school in 1948. After attending Scottsbluff Junior College for one year, he enlisted in the U.S. Navy. He served his country for three years during the Korean conflict aboard an aircraft carrier, the USS Boxer, and later was stationed on the Island of Guam fulfilling his assignment with Special Services. After four years, he was honorably discharged from the Navy and returned home. He finished his education at Scottsbluff Jr. College and went into business with his father, who owned and operated The Scottsbluff Tent and Awning Company.

Bill and I asked Papa to officiate at our wedding and asked him to check his church calendar for a date over the holidays. I had always dreamed of having my wedding over the Christmas holidays. We agreed on New Year's Eve for our wedding date and were so excited and excitedly began making plans for that special day. The last day of the year was to be OUR day.

* * *

My sister Eva and Johannes Grohmann set their wedding date for November 25, 1955. Two of the Wilhelm daughters were to be married within one month's time. I know my parents were very disappointed and sad not to be able to attend Eva's wedding and so were her siblings.

At the same time I was very disappointed that I would not have my oldest sister present at my wedding; again there was the familiar separation that plagued our family.

My parents got acquainted with Art and Caroline Osborn, Bill's parents, as well as Bill's sister, Donna Walters, who lived in Scottsbluff. I remember Carrie (the name Bill's mom went by) and Donna were invited to our house one afternoon for coffee to discuss wedding plans with my mother and me. Donna had two children, Ozzie and Sandy, whom we asked to be in our wedding as ring bearer and flower girl. As was customary here, I had several bridal showers after our wedding was announced. We received many lovely gifts and were very grateful for the generosity of our family and friends.

* * *

I was very fortunate to have two of my siblings in our wedding party. My sister, Esther, and her fiancé, Don Klett, made plans to come from Chicago. My brother Fred, who was stationed at Lowry Air-force base in Denver where he was in Tech training, also planned on attending our wedding.

That made me very happy.

Bill's best friend, Elton Gillam, who lived in California, was to be best man and my sister Esther was to be my Maid of Honor. I asked Jeanne Brown, my dear friend, to be my bridesmaid and my brother Fred was asked to be our groomsman.

Mutti spent many hours making my wedding dress. It was a white gown, styled with a Chantilly lace fitted bodice, featuring long pointed sleeves and a mandarin collar. The floor length, full skirt was net over satin. It was very pretty and I was very proud of my mother for having made it. Mutti and I shopped for a veil and found one we both liked which was suitable for my dress. It was a fingertip veil of illusion held in place by a crown of pearls.

Planning our wedding was a very exciting time in my life.

The Osborn families were very committed, and active members of the United Methodist Church in

Scottsbluff where Bill was baptized and confirmed, but Bill agreed to be married in my church. The Reverend K.M. Wilhelm, my father, performed the double ring ceremony on December 31, 1955, at the Zion Evangelical Lutheran Church in Scottsbluff.

About 150 guests witnessed the 2 o'clock afternoon nuptial rites.

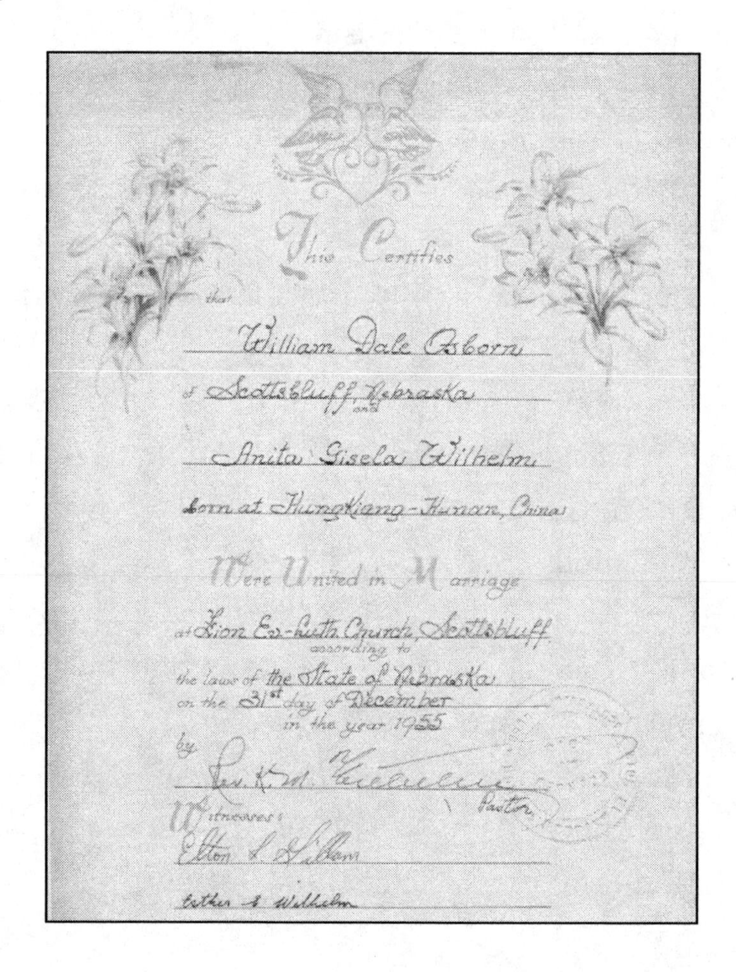

This Certifies

that

William Dale Osborn

of Scottsbluff, Nebraska

and

Anita Gisela Wilhelm

born at Hungkiang-Hunan, China

Were United in Marriage

at Zion Ev.-Luth. Church, Scottsbluff

according to

the law of the State of Nebraska

on the 31st day of December

in the year 1955

by

Rev. K.M. Wilhelm

Pastor

Witnesses:

Elton L. Gillem

Esther A. Wilhelm

American and German traditions were combined at the ceremony with the wedding party walking down the isle as couples. Since my father performed the ceremony and I had no one to give me away, we followed the German tradition and walked down the isle as a couple, following the ring bearer and flower girl. The Best Man and Maid of Honor, as well as the Bridesmaid and the Groomsman, followed the Bride and Groom. A wedding reception in the church parlor followed the ceremony.

* * *

Later that evening Bill and I left on our wedding trip to Denver and other Colorado points of interest. A severe snowstorm interrupted our travels and forced us to stay in Cheyenne, Wyoming for the first night. We stayed at a Guest Ranch Motel that had wonderful accommodations.

The next morning we left Cheyenne and drove to Ft. Collins, Colorado, where Bill's aunt and uncle were expecting us. We had dinner with Dr. and Mrs. Fred Humphrey and their son Robert, and I enjoyed meeting them very much. Aunt Vi was one of Bill's father's six sisters and I was drawn to her immediately.

Later that afternoon we drove to Denver where we had reservations in a nice motel. We saw many interesting sights and visited several museums. One day we drove to Central City and had fun exploring that old city and hiking around the Colorado mountainside.

We returned to Scottsbluff after spending a wonderful week in Colorado and moved into our first apartment on Second Avenue.

15

The Years of 1955-1965

Later that year we moved into a little house on an acreage that Bill purchased after he was discharged from the Navy with money he had saved during his four years in the service. The house was small, but it was ours, and we loved it. Adjacent to our house was a big yard and a place for Bill's horses and a barn. We also had several dogs and a nanny goat. It was a new experience for me to be surrounded by animals. They often did not please me, especially when the nanny goat got into my garden and ate my vegetables, or when the dogs barked early in the morning, waking us from a deep sleep. Bill loved his horses and his hunting dogs and because I loved him, I tried very hard to get used to living in a country setting. Bill belonged to the Scottsbluff Saddle Club and he often took part in the club's activities. I loved watching my handsome "Cowboy" ride his horse, which he did well. To please Bill, I rode a horse sometimes, but was never very comfortable or self confident in the saddle.

Bill was also an avid hunter and loved being out in the fields with his dog, watching him point and retrieve pheasants for him. He often took the game he brought home from a hunting trip to my father who loved eating it.

After Bill finished his second year at the Junior College, he decided to work in his father's business full time, hoping to expand and improve the company by modernizing the operation. Bill's father was not easy to work for, but Bill was determined to be successful in his business venture and tried his best to gain his fathers respect. His salary was minimal and I worked at the hospital to supplement our income. We often struggled to make ends meet, but it did not occur to us that we were poor or deter us from living a happy life.

Being confident that hard work and faith would pay off at the end, we were happy to be together and carried on to the best of our abilities.

Bill promised Papa that as long as he was ministering in the Zion Church we would be attending services there, which we did. However, Papa preached one Sunday in English and one in German and since Bill did not speak or understand the German language, he only attended English services. On holidays Papa preached half of the service in English and the other half in German, which resulted in a long service, but it was the best solution for bilingual church services.

* * *

My brother Hans, who followed in his father's footsteps and became a missionary, lived in Taiwan, Formosa. He met and fell in love with a young secretary named Alice Bell, from Canada, who was also doing mission work in Formosa. They married on March 10, 1956, but unfortunately without any family members present. Such were the sacrifices with which missionaries were confronted.

* * *

My first pregnancy was very difficult and our oldest son, Steven Michael, was born prematurely and arrived very unexpectedly. He was so tiny and weighed only 4 lb. 6 oz. when we brought him home from the hospital. Actually, we stayed with Bill's parents for a while, until we felt that we could handle our newborn by ourselves. My own mother was visiting in Germany during this time, and I missed having her with me to share in my joy of our baby, her first grandchild.

My sister Esther was living in Scottsbluff during the summer of 1956 and worked at General Hospital as a registered nurse. She was present when my baby was born and was such a comfort and support to me; I was so grateful for having her with me and loved being able to share the special experience of my son's birth with her.

* * *

Stevie, as we called him, had a very difficult start in life. He was allergic to all dairy products and it was a real challenge for us to find a formula that agreed with him. We adored him and he was our pride and joy. Dr. Lovett assured us that in time he would outgrow his allergies, but he stated that it could take up to six years for him to catch up physically with other children his age. Before he was three years old, he had contracted about every known childhood disease and had a tonsillectomy to eliminate the frequent infections of his throat.

Stevie was a very sweet natured and sensitive child and developed into a very bright and happy little boy. He loved books early in his child development, and we read to him every day, especially at bedtime.

In November of 1956, Stevie took his first trip with his parents and grandparents when we traveled to Chicago to attend the wedding of my sister Esther and Don Klett. My father officiated at the wedding, and I was her matron of honor. My sister Peggie traveled to Chicago from Washington D.C. to be her sister's bridesmaid. It was a wonderful wedding and a very memorable occasion. Stevie met his Aunt Peggie for the first time and called her "Aunt Piggy". He associated her name with a stuffed toy pig that she had brought to him for a gift.

My brother Fred was in basic training in Lockland Air Force Base in San Antonio, Texas and was unable to attend Esther's wedding. Later, he was stationed in Germany and had the opportunity to see his sister Eva numerous times.

In February of 1957, I wrote the following in a letter to my Aunt Hedel Richter in Germany: "We are all well! Bill is such a good husband to me and a wonderful father to our little son, Stevie. We are such a happy little family. Bill and I understand each other perfectly and I want you to know that I would not have been able to find a better husband in Germany. I firmly believe that God had His plan, when he led me to America and to Scottsbluff where I met my future husband. Stevie is doing well and is such a joy to us. Bill is so very proud of his son. Mutti and Papa are crazy about their first little grandchild and love to be with him"...

* * *

It was an Osborn tradition to have every Sunday dinner at Grandmas house; her fried chicken and mashed potatoes were a family favorite.

Bill's sister Donna, her husband Chuck Walters, and their three children, Ozzie, Sandra and Jimmy lived in Scottsbluff and we often shared Sunday dinners together.

The American slang was often difficult for me to decipher and gave me problems from time to time. Months after we were married, I asked Bill one time to explain the meaning of S.O.B to me, which he did. I had used that phrase one time while I was working at the hospital, thinking that it had the same meaning as "son of a gun". But how wrong I was... The girls I worked with went into hysterics when they heard me, but wouldn't, or couldn't explain the meaning to me. I asked my father, but he wasn't sure of it. We scanned the dictionary, but were unable to find it there either. Papa said: "From now on, don't use any such phrases if you don't know the meaning of them." So I was very careful from that time on, not to use any American slang words or phrases.

Bill's sister Donna invited me to join a Project Club soon after we were married, and I enjoyed learning all sorts of crafts and being with other young women.

One night someone asked me if I had problems learning the English language, to which I replied: "No, the language came very easily to me, but I did have problems learning American slang. For instance, I did not know what an S.O.B. was until I married Bill." That remark absolutely brought the house down and everyone roared with laughter at what I had said. Of course what I meant was that Bill was able to explain the meaning of that horrible phrase to me. I was mortified, to say the least.

In 1958 I had the wonderful opportunity of becoming a naturalized citizen of the United States. It was such a thrill for me to join the ranks of being an American. America became my country as well as my home, and I was so proud of it.

I came to this country to be reunited with my family, but I came for another reason also. That reason was to live in a country where I could be free. I felt that Americans took their freedom much too lightly. Having grown up in Hitler's Nazi Germany and living under the Russian Oppression behind the iron curtain made me appreciate the new freedom that I gained here in America.

Before I was able to apply for my United States Citizenship, I had to take a course in American history and government, as well as a 36-hour class in citizenship. It was a very interesting experience and I met other immigrants who desired to become U.S. citizens.

Dr. Lovett and Max Coppom graciously agreed to be my sponsors, and Judge Richard Van Steenberg was the presiding judge over the swearing in ceremony.

Ten persons took the oath of United States Citizenship at the final naturalization proceedings in Scottsbluff County District Court.

Following the administration of the citizen oath, Judge Van Steenberg explained the responsibilities and privileges that go with U.S. Citizenship.

A nice reception followed the ceremony where the new citizens were greeted by their families and friends.

It was an unforgettable experience for me.

* * *

Our second son arrived in May of 1959 and we named him Donald Bryan. To prevent another premature birth, I had to have complete bed rest during the last three months of my pregnancy, which was difficult with a toddler in the house. Mutti and Grandma Osborn took turns keeping Stevie during the day and also helped out with the meals. Donald weighed 6lb and 4 oz. and was a healthy baby. From day one he was a spunky little guy and so adorable.

Stevie adored his little brother and showed no jealousy at all. We were so grateful and thankful to God for giving us these two precious little boys, and we loved them from the bottom of our hearts.

When Donnie was only a few months old and Stevie was three years old, we took a trip to Arkansas to visit my sister Esther and her husband Don who was studying architecture in Silom Springs, Arkansas. Bill's mother traveled with us as far as Kansas where we left her to visit her relatives

Carrie was a remarkable woman and a wonderful mother-in-law. I loved her very much. She was very kind and supportive to me in every way and adored her grandchildren.

Carrie's growing-up years were spent in southeastern Kansas where her parents had settled and raised a large family. Her father, John Albert Christopher and her mother, Caroline Smith Craig Christopher, were both born in Jersey County, Illinois where they grew up, met, fell in love and were married on September 3, 1884. Two years later the couple moved to Hugoton, Kansas. The sheer vastness of the prairies must have been overwhelming to them. John

Christopher homesteaded and accumulated a substantial amount of farm and ranchland. In his later years he was considered one of the most prominent landowners in West Center Township, Kansas. They endured drought, scorching winds, blizzards, prairie fires and grasshopper invasions, and still they persevered. The couple was blessed with seven children. They, too, knew the rigors of pioneer life and were assigned responsibilities at an early age.

This generation was a sturdy group of survivors as well. In the 30's, while they were establishing their own homes and families, they had to endure the depression and lived through the era of the dust bowl days.

Carrie became a registered pharmacist and worked in her profession until she moved to Scottsbluff, Nebraska to marry Arthur Elmer Osborn, Bill's father.

The couple met on a blind date while Carrie was visiting a friend in Scottsbluff, and after a very short courtship they were married at the Methodist Church in Denver, Colorado.

Mom, was very close to her family and took every opportunity to visit them in Kansas. She was especially close to her sister Ella, who was unmarried and still lived in the family home. We had a wonderful family get-together while we were in Hugoton and I met many, many relatives.

While the family was eating and having a great time visiting with one another, little Stevie got bored and decided to get on with the trip. He knew that we were headed to see his Aunt Esther. His little suitcase in hand, he started walking along the highway by himself. We were very frightened when we discovered that our little boy was missing and several of the family members started driving in different directions looking for him. Much to Stevie's dismay, he was picked up and brought back to the family. His father gave him a good lesson after that episode and told him to never take off by himself again.

We had a great time on the rest of the trip to Arkansas and I loved seeing my sister again.

In the fall of 1959 Bill had the opportunity to purchase "The Sterling Tent and Awning Company" in Sterling, Colorado. We began a new adventure and moved to Sterling, Colorado. Bill was excited to have a business of his own and worked very hard to develop this company and create a successful operation.

We purchased a house in a nice neighborhood, made new friends in this new town and enjoyed living there. We especially liked living close to Denver and to the mountains that we loved. We took advantage of our location by taking many weekend trips to the Colorado Rockies.

* * *

My father resigned his position as Pastor from the Zion Church in Scottsbluff in 1960 after serving the church for almost ten years. He was commissioned by the Liebenzell Mission Headquarter in Wuertenberg, Germany to serve on the mission board, become a staff member and visit mission fields in Japan and Formosa from time to time.

They were delighted to move back to Germany, their homeland for a few years.

My sister Eva, who lived in Germany with her family, was thrilled with the prospect of being able to spend time with her parents. It was wonderful for them to be able to get acquainted with her children.

Mutti and Papa visited us in Sterling before they left on their journey, and we took them to the airport in Denver, saying good-bye to them once again.

* * *

Our two little boys were growing up and were such a precious gift to us. We focused on keeping them healthy and happy. Bill's business where he worked hard and put in long hours was doing well, and I enjoyed being a stay-at-home mom.

I remember being invited to a Mother-Daughter banquet in Church and longed to have a daughter of my own when I saw so many mothers with their little girls.

My wish was granted in 1961 when our darling little daughter was born. She too was born early and was very tiny and petite, weighing 5lb and 4 oz.

Her birth date was December 9 and we called her our Christmas present. What a special gift we had in our baby girl. Jenny was a beautiful baby and I can still see her propped up in her little infant seat sitting under our Christmas tree.

Her brothers were so proud of their little sister.

* * *

My sister Peggie came from Washington D.C. to celebrate Christmas with us, and we had a wonderful time together. She derived a lot of enjoyment from dressing Jenny in cute little outfits and carrying her around the house.

One morning while Jenny was sleeping in her little basket, Stevie brought his neighbor friend in to show off his little sister. His friend took a peak at her and said: "I will come back when her eyes are open." We had a good laugh over that remark...

When Jenny was just a few months old, a local businessman wanted to buy "The Sterling Tent and Awning Company" approached Bill and made him a good offer to purchase his business. My husband took advantage of this timely opportunity and sold his company. Art Osborn, Bill's father, had decided to retire and offered to sell Bill his company in Scottsbluff. After living in Colorado for about two years we moved back home to Scottsbluff. It seemed like the right choice for us and although I would like to have stayed in Colorado, Bill was drawn back to his hometown.

So, in the spring of 1962, Bill and I, with our three little children, moved to Scottsbluff where Bill became the owner of the "Scottsbluff Tent and Awning Company." We were happy to be among family and old friends again, and made many new friends in a "Newcomers Club" that we joined. We learned to play bridge while living in Sterling and discovered that playing bridge was as popular here as it had been there. It was a wonderful way to get acquainted with newcomers in the community and provided interesting and inexpensive entertainment.

* * *

My beloved grandfather, Oskar Wilhelm, died on May 27, 1962. He was 92 years old and had been widowed for 14 years. The last time I saw him was 12 years previously when I said farewell to him at the train-station in Aue. He died on Donnie's 3rd birthday. I mourned him deeply.

* 15. 8. 1870 † 27. 5. 1962

2. Tim. 4, 7 u. 8

Unser lieber Vater

OSKAR WILHELM

ist im Alter von 92 Jahren heimgegangen.

In stiller Trauer

Seine dankbaren Kinder

Zschorlau/Erzgeb., am 28. Mai 1962

Die Beerdigung findet am Freitag, dem 1. Juni 1962, 14.00 Uhr, statt.

The traditional German "Death Notice" for my Grandfather, sent to family and friends.

* * *

Later that summer we started building a house on land that we owned just outside of Scottsbluff's city limit. The acreage was subdivided into lots with the purpose of creating a housing development. We built our house on one of the lots. It was a very challenging and interesting learning experience and we enjoyed watching every step of the building process. The house had three bedrooms, living room, dining area with a kitchen, bathroom and a full basement that Bill finished himself a couple of years later. We were very excited to move into this lovely house and worked hard to make it our home. We felt so blessed!

While Bill was very focused on his business, I enjoyed being home with our children. I liked sewing for them and made many of the clothes they wore. I remember making little pleated skirts for Jenny, using Pendleton shirts that had worn out collars and sleeves. The idea came from sewing tips that were used during the war. Worn out coats were ripped apart and the back of the fabric was used to create new coats. I wore several such coats while growing up. It was a very practical and creative way to recycle old merchandise, when new merchandise was unavailable.

* * *

In the late summer of that year we decided to take a camping trip to Yellowstone National Park, taking the two little boys and leaving Jenny with her Grandma

Osborn. We were all packed, and the necessary food was prepared when we found out that our car was malfunctioning. The small part that was needed to repair the car was not available in Scottsbluff, but could be purchased in Cheyenne, Wyoming. Leonard Cook, who was one of Bill's employees, offered to fly Bill to Cheyenne in his small, two-passenger "Aeronica Champ" airplane, to obtain the needed part for the car. The children and I were eagerly waiting for Bill's return from Cheyenne, when the phone call came that the plane had crashed on a ranch, near Cheyenne. It's two passengers walked away from the crash, but the plane was totaled. It was a very scary experience for us, and needless to say, we canceled our trip. God spared Bill's life! For that we were unbelievably grateful.

* * *

We joined the Methodist Church, the church that Bill grew up in and felt very welcome and happy with our new church home. We took the children to Sunday school and I joined the Chancel Choir. Our choir director was Mr. R.J. Roberts and I greatly enjoyed singing under his direction.

At the same time I joined a community choral group that went by the name of "Platte Valley Oratorio

Society." The members of the choir represented singers from all walks of life. The only prerequisite for membership was a love for quality music and a desire to sing. I loved singing classical music and choir rehearsals were one of my favorite hours of the week. The Platte Valley Oratorio Society performed two concerts yearly and I was very proud to be part of this fine organization.

* * *

The Christmas holiday was always a very special time at our house and with our family. Bill and I agreed that we would combine American and German Christmas traditions and it worked out well. It was my wish that my children learn about the wonderful traditions that I grew up with in the "Erzgebirg" mountains in Germany. Bill and I received many Christmas decorations as wedding gifts from my German relatives. Decorations such as pyramids, carved angels and miners with candles, an advent star, as well as nutcrackers that we treasured. We always celebrated the first of Advent by lighting the first candle on our Advent wreath and as the children got older, they got to light the candles. Closer to Christmas we decorated our home with evergreen boughs and holly, and of course our German decorations. I made white paper stars that I learned to make when I was a little girl and we even put real candles on our tree. I always baked "Springerle" cookies that were a Christmas specialty, as well as other baked goods. The festivities began on Christmas Eve. We had a light supper before we attended the candlelight service at our church that was always very inspirational with beautiful music and the word of God, reminding us of the true meaning of Christmas, the birth of Christ.

The children couldn't wait to get home to open their presents. Anticipation and excitement filled the air until every last package had been opened and admired. The best present to Bill and me was the glow on our children's faces. On Christmas morning the children found their stockings filled with goodies from Santa and were so excited that Santa had come to our house, but how? Santa was never emphasized or of great importance in our home, but we included him in our traditional Christmas celebration.

Christmas day we spent with our parents, at their house or ours. It would not have been Christmas without the traditional roast goose and red cabbage that I prepared when we had dinner at our house.

* * *

In March of 1963, Papa came to visit us for a few days. He was coming from Japan, via Portland, where he visited Esther and her family. It was the first time that he saw our little Jenny who was now two years old. We had a wonderful time together and I felt that Papa really enjoyed our family. He seemed very comfortable in our home and with Bill and me. I was so thrilled when I read the entry he wrote into our guest book.

Coming from Japan - Los Angeles - Portland
I had the joy to stay here a few days. I saw
for the first Jennifer and enjoyed the happy
life of the family. Thank you for all you
gave me: time and affection. God
will richly reward + bless you and
the children.
Scottsbluff, March 23. - 29. 1963
Papa Wilhelm
Phil. 1:6

* * *

Our son Steven (his name in school) was enrolled at Bryant grade school and was doing very well. He was a very serious and conscientious student and received good grades and reports from his teachers; school came very easy for him. At home the two little brothers played together a lot, but Donnie was always the more aggressive one. Several times he fell and cut himself, requiring stitches, but that did not keep him from actively engaging in activity that were often unsafe. His older brother was much more cautious and careful in his actions and looked out for his younger brother.

We lived close to the "Riverside Zoo" and often heard the lion's roar, to the delight of the children, who knew they were caged in and not roaming free. The Zoo had a nice area for picnics, and we frequently ate our suppers in one of the shelters there. The "Wild Cat Hills," a beautiful wooded and hilly area south of Gering, was another favorite spot for family outings in our valley. We hiked and picnicked there, alone, or with friends and always had a great time.

* * *

My parents informed us in late 1964 that their time in Germany was coming to an end and asked us to look for a little house for them to buy in our neighborhood.

Papa said they wanted to be "within shouting distance" away from our house; and were eager to see our children grow up, having missed being with me during my growing-up years. We were thrilled at the prospect of having Mutti and Papa close to us and started searching for the right house for them immediately. A nice house became available just a block away from our house; it was just perfect for my parents and suited them to a tee. Bill and I, along with some of our friends, renovated the house, installed new draperies, painted every wall and made it very livable for Mutti and Papa. Their furniture and other belongings were stored in the garage of a house in Greeley, Colorado, which my parents had purchased before they left for Germany and used for a rental property. The rental house was sold and their belongings moved to Scottsbluff into their new home.

The house was ready to move into, linens and towels were put in place and the pantry and refrigerator were stocked with food. We even planted flowers in the front yard to welcome Mutti and Papa back to Scottsbluff.

We were so excited and couldn't wait until their arrival from Germany. It was in the spring of 1965 when they moved into their home and it met with their approval; they loved it, and that made us very happy.

The children were so happy to have Mutti and Papa living close to us and visited them often.

Afternoon "coffee time" is a tradition for German people and my parents held that tradition in high regard. It was a wonderful break for me in the afternoon to go to their house for coffee, along with the children and Bill, when he was able to. Mutti's "Pflaumenkuchen," (plum coffee cake) was Bill's favorite of Mutti's pastries and he always made sure to be there when she served it.

It was wonderful to see Papa relaxed, without church duties or church members to counsel. He loved watching "Jeopardy" on television and wouldn't miss that show for anything. Often Mutti and Papa walked to our house for a visit, or a meal, or just to be with the children. I must say that the time after my parents came back from Germany was one of the happiest times with them and I treasure those special memories. Papa liked to talk about his childhood in Zschorlau and the relatives there, but never talked much about China, or, their decision to leave me with my grandparents. In retrospect, I know that perhaps I should have initiated bringing these old issues to the surface, but the fear of rejection was too great to bring to light. It was more comfortable to just focus on the present.

* * *

After the birth of her third daughter, my sister Esther was diagnosed with ovarian cancer. It was a great shock to the whole family, especially my parents. Surgery was performed and we were assured that her prognosis was quite good and we were very hopeful and confident that Esther would be all right.

16

Coming Home - Family Reunion

The fact that my parents never had the joy of having all six of their children united together at one time with them, was often talked about. It was their greatest wish to have a family reunion. On the eve of their seventieth birthdays in December of 1965, Bill and I decided to bring it about and gather all of my siblings from near and far to make this reunion a reality. They literally came from all over the world to be in Scottsbluff with our parents and each other. My oldest sister Eva came from Germany, her first trip to the U.S. since she left ten years earlier; my brother Hans and his wife Alice and their two children, Marty and Lita, came from California; my sister Esther and husband Don Klett and their three daughters, Donna, Laurie and Karla came from Chicago; brother Fred came from Portland and my sister Peggie arrived from Washington D.C. Of course Bill and I and our three children, Steve, Donnie and Jenny were living here in Scottsbluff. Nineteen family members gathered at this unique family experience and we were able to spend several unforgettable days together. My parent's wish was finally fulfilled and we all felt a deep sense of accomplishment to have made the effort to complete this venture. We were very grateful that God allowed us to have the reunion of our family. It was to be the FIRST and ONLY time that the Wilhelm family would be united here on Earth.

17
Osborn Family Life

Bill and I had been married for ten years now and they were happy years. Our children were such a joy to us and developed beautifully. Steve and Donnie both attended Bryant grade school, the same school Bill went to as a young child, and were doing very well. They both were in Cub Scouts and enjoyed its activities. I was a Den Mother in Cub Scouts and Bill was a Webelos leader; we both enjoyed our respective roles.

Steve showed a keen interest in music early in his childhood and started taking piano lessons when he was eight years old. He loved music and progressed very quickly. Bill signed Steve up in a baseball league and he played ball for one summer, but preferred piano lessons over baseball the next summer. We discovered early on raising our children that we must honor and listen to their preferences, likes and dislikes and support them in all of their endeavors.

Donnie was an entertainer from the time he was very young. He loved standing on a table, or a platform to sing for anyone who would listen. He loved making costumes for himself and was great at improvising with whatever was available. I remember a Pilgrim costume he made one year for Thanksgiving, complete with top hat and buckled shoes. One Christmas season we took the children to the Y.M.C.A. children's Christmas party and after many little groups had performed for the audience, the M.C. asked if there was anyone in the audience who would like to perform. To his parent's surprise, Donnie raised his little hand and said; "I would like to sing Jingle Bells." The M.C. said, "You just come right on up to the stage." Little Donnie Osborn did, and sang his Christmas song flawlessly; he was four and a half years old.

We experienced, as many parents do, that there is never a dull moment with children. I remember so well what happened one Sunday morning when Jenny was about five years old. My choir sang at the early Church Service and I went alone while Bill was staying at home to get the children fed and ready for Sunday school. While he was busy preparing breakfast, little Jenny left the house unnoticed and took off to walk to Grandma Osborn's house, which was located about one mile from our house. An elderly lady who saw her walking along the street by herself invited her to come into her house for a cookie. While Jenny was gleefully eating her cookie, the lady called the police to report this unattended child, who obviously walked away from home. When the police officer arrived and questioned our little girl she simply told him that she wanted to go to her Grandma's house; the officer took her the remaining distance and was happy to deliver her to her destination.

In the meantime, Bill was frantic and started looking for her and was extremely relieved when he learned that his little girl was at his parent's house. We were very grateful that we lived in a small community and not in a big city.

* * *

It was during that year that I met a young woman who had also come from Germany some years earlier. Her name was Erika Hawkins and we soon became very well acquainted, enjoying each other's company. One day while we were playing bridge, Erika and I sat at the same game table and were asked when we came from Germany. During the conversation we learned that Erika and I had left Germany the same year, the same day and on the same ship; what a small world it is that we live in. We were absolutely astounded.

Erika's husband Doug was the manager of "Magnolia Mobile Homes Company," a factory that manufactured mobile homes. He approached Bill one day with the prospect of making draperies for his mobile homes as a sideline of his "Tent and Awning Company." Bill was always ready for expansion and new challenges, and agreed to pursue this new venture. With the help of Doug Hawkins, Bill started the new division of his company and focused very hard on learning the drapery business. This was the beginning of a business that lasted until our retirement.

* * *

One year later, Bill developed another division of his business that produced insulated floor panels that were used in the manufacturing of mobile homes. The panels were of high quality insulation, insect, as well as waterproof, and were very light in weight. The product proved to be very successful for the manufacturing of expandable mobile homes.

* * *

In the fall of 1966, my sister Esther's cancer reappeared and after two more surgeries it became apparent that her condition was grave and worsening. What a devastating blow to the whole family. Mutti and Papa made the decision to travel to Chicago to be with Esther and her family during the final weeks of her life.

Her husband Don was grief stricken and it was difficult for him to cope with three little girls and a very ill wife. The next few weeks Esther was in and out of the hospital, but she was very courageous, and knew the reality of her situation. She wrote the following letter to her siblings on December 17, 1966:

> *Dear Brothers and Sisters,*
>
> *It is with a little difficulty that I am writing this letter. I've been so grateful that Papa has been so faithful in keeping you all informed at this time. I appreciate so much your cards, letters and above all the prayers for us as a family. Even though we don't know what the Lord's plans are for us, we thank Him for the peace in our hearts and for the assurance of His Presence and love.*
>
> *Papa returned from Scottsbluff today. Don and the girls met him at the train. Mutti has been such a help and blessing. How good of the Lord to allow Mutti and Papa to be here at this time and for giving them health and strength. Don has been so good with the girls; they think the world of their Daddy anyway.*

I've been home for three weeks now and have been to see the Doctor weekly to receive an injection for the cancer. However, gradually the pains have been increasing, the appetite failing and the nausea increasing. The doctor told me today that I have to return to the hospital. We are hoping that it is only for a few days of intravenous feedings and getting the intestines to function properly again.

It is hard to leave the home again just one week before Christmas, but the Lord sees all this and He cares. Don put up a beautiful Christmas tree several days ago and I've enjoyed it as well as all of our Christmas records.

Friends have been writing and dropping in. I'd so wish I could see all of you once more. Anita and Bill are planning to come on December 27th and stay a few days. Nucki hopes to come in January. Only the Lord knows whether this is my last letter or not. I'm looking forward to seeing Him face to face. My prayer also is that each one of you will join me some day, as well as each of the children.

May the Lord become very precious to all of you at this time.

All our Love,

Esther

This was indeed Esther's last letter. Bill and I flew to Chicago and were able to see her one last time. She was so brave and never complained or questioned her lot in life. She totally accepted the Lord's will and was ready to meet him.

Esther died on January 27th, 1967 at the age of 33 years, leaving her husband and three little daughters behind. Mutti and Papa, as well as the whole family mourned her death deeply.

* * *

I so often thought of my sister Esther and of her gentle, yet determined way of handling life's situations. She was truly a wonderful example of a committed Christian and at her young age had accomplished so much. My heart ached and I felt a deep bereavement of losing my sister after only knowing her for such a short time...

* * *

It was in the spring of 1967 that the Scottsbluff High School music department performed "Oliver," a musical adaptation of Oliver Twist. Steve was in 5th Grade and was chosen to play one of the boys in the Musical. It was a wonderful learning experience for him, and we enjoyed watching him on stage with such pride in our hearts. I remember getting special seats for Mutti and Papa to sit in the front row to watch their grandson perform. It was the first Musical they ever attended and they enjoyed it immensely.

* * *

Papa preached in several churches in the valley during that time, filling in for vacationing pastors, or, those who were otherwise unable to fill their pulpit.

Preaching fulfilled his need for ministering to congregations who were without a pastor.

His concern during these months, however, was that his eyesight was failing him and that he might not be able to drive his car much longer.

* * *

It was his greatest wish to return to his homeland of Germany, one last time, and he spoke of it frequently. He discussed it with Mutti who wanted no part of it. The wound of losing her beloved daughter Esther was so fresh and she feared having to re-live the last days of Esther's life with all the relatives in Germany, as well as friends with whom she would come in contact. She had not yet healed from the shock of Esther's death and wanted to stay home to accomplish that.

One day Papa arrived home with airline tickets for Germany, and thus the plan for the trip was sealed. They decided to stop in Washington, D.C. to see their youngest daughter, Peggie, and to meet her husband Walter and their little grandson Bryan, whom they had not met before. Peggy had married Walter Markowich in 1966 in Washington D.C.

* * *

Little did we know when my parents left for their trip that we would not see Papa again. While traveling in East and West Germany, my parents were able to see many relatives and friends and sent us letters and post cards with glowing reports of the great time they were having.

They spent more than three months visiting their home country and spending much quality time with Eva and her family in Ludwigshafen. Papa and Mutti departed Germany and flew back to New York on October 13, 1967. While they were passing through the passport checkpoint Papa suddenly collapsed, lost consciousness and immediately was rushed to a nearby hospital but his heart had already stopped when the ambulance arrived. It was an unbelievable shock for my mother and it was remarkable how well she coped with the situation. Friends from Schooley's Mountain, the mission headquarter of the Liebenzell Mission in New Jersey, were waiting for their arrival and came to Mutti's rescue. They were such a godsend and we were so grateful for their help and the comfort Mutti found with the Mission Home family.

* * *

It was evening in Scottsbluff, and we were waiting for a call from Papa informing us of their safe arrival back in the United States. Instead of Papa calling, it was Mutti who gave us the news of Papa's sudden departure and home going. What a devastating shock that was, to the children and us. We were told that Papa's remains would not be brought back to

Scottsbluff, but instead, that he would be buried in Hackettstown, New Jersey, near Schooley's Mountain. My parents had always planned on moving to Schooley's Mountain eventually to spend their golden years with their missionary friends at the home of the Liebenzell Mission. So it came to no surprise to us that Mutti wanted to have Papa buried there. Arrangements were made for the funeral at Schooley's Mountain on October 17, 1967.

Bill and I made plans to fly to New Jersey to be with Mutti as soon as possible, and to attend Papa's services. My brother Hans and his family were doing Mission work in San Paulo, Brazil and were not able to come, neither was my sister Eva from Germany. Brother Fred, who lived in Portland and sister Peggie and husband from Washington, D.C., as well as our brother-in-law Don Klett from Chicago, came to Schooley's Mountain to be at Mutti's side, and to say their farewell to Papa. The Service was a wonderful tribute to my father and was very comforting for the family. The scripture readings and texts for the service were Revelations 14:13 "Blessed are the dead who die in the Lord" and

Matthew 25:21 "His Master said to him, 'Well done, good and faithful servant; you have been faithful over a little, I will set you over much; enter into the joy of your Master.'"

Papa had completed his mission here on earth and was finally at home, with his daughter Esther who had preceded him in death just a few short months earlier.

Bill and I brought Mutti home with us to Scottsbluff and she settled in to her home on Park View Lane. Being alone, without Papa, was quite an adjustment for my mother and she had to cope with many things that were new to her. She had never written a check before, nor did she drive a car. We were very grateful that we were living close to her and could be at her beck and call when she needed help. The children often spent time with Mutti after school, or on weekends, and Jenny spend many nights with her to keep her company. We had many meals together and she still liked to bake and have us over for coffee and one of her good pastries. Zion Church was still the church she attended and she had several friends there who were very good to her, picking her up for church functions or taking her out to lunch at times. She really enjoyed that.

* * *

I had started an "At Home Business" some time earlier by doing Custom Sewing and had several regular clients and loved creating garments for them, mostly derived from "Vogue Patterns." I made several new dresses and outfits for Mutti and she enjoyed wearing them; for the first time she visited a Beauty Shop and was so proud of her new hairdo. Bill finished our basement some time before I started sewing, and built a wonderful sewing room for me. It had a long fold out table that I used for cutting out patterns, a long mirror and a good and a well-lit area for my sewing machine. I spent many hours in that room while the children were at school and loved it; it was truly my therapy. I don't believe I possessed any garment in my wardrobe that I didn't make myself, and I often made outfits for Jenny to match mine. It was such fun to have mother-daughter outfits to wear to Church or other places. Jenny was a very petite little girl and had such a sweet nature. She had many little friends to play with, but her most special friend was her imaginary friend that she called "Gaga." She held very interesting and long conversations with her in her room that made us chuckle, but she was very serious about it.

Steve started violin lessons while he was in the fifth grade and enjoyed his new challenge. When he was attending the 7th Grade he had a violin solo during an orchestra concert at the Junior High School. He did very well, but Mom and Dad were shaking in their boots when their little guy walked across that big stage.

* * *

It was during that time that one of the television networks showed a program that was called "Combat." I had a real adversity to that show because it presented a very negative and weak side of the German soldiers. Among many other reasons, we instructed our children not to watch that show on T.V. One night while Bill and I were out, a baby-sitter was taking care of our children and she let them watch "Combat." The next morning while we were still in bed, Donnie came to our room and gleefully told us that we should have been home to watch "Combat" with them because it had no German soldiers in the show, only "Krauts."

* * *

Mutti received many old letters and documents from the Liebenzell Mission's archive; one of the records was in the form of a recorded tape that Mutti was quite anxious to hear. The recording contained the Biographical Sketch of my father Karl Max Wilhelm as presented by the Liebenzell Mission. The following is a quote from this recording:

When, in the beginning of 1935, the return of the Wilhelm family to China came under discussion, the leadership committee of the Mission strongly urged my parents to take only three children with them to China and to leave two at home in Germany.

My parents responded to this matter as follows:

Yesterday we received your kind letter of January 2 and want to express our sincere thanks. Often the uncertainty of the past month became a heavy burden for us. In spite of the nebulous future facing us, we are glad nevertheless once again to have a concrete goal before us. We are very clear in our own minds, that we are facing an unsure and dangerous future. We are not driven by enthusiasm, because we have spent far too many years in China and have come to know the realities and serious aspects of missionary work.

We are thankful to you, that even during this time of difficulty you have expressed your confidence in us to send us once again to the mission field. As much as lies in us, we will endeavor with God's help to show ourselves worthy of this confidence. We can only walk by faith the path, which lies before us. We are further confident that we are on the right path before God, even if the mission leadership cannot provide us with any other guarantees than the unfailing promises of the Word of God. From the human perspective, our hearts might tremble and fear. There is a constant tension of trust and faith - but the assurance of our "mission" (that we are sent by God) remains our source of strength.

Since there is no question that our return to the mission field is a matter of stepping out in faith, we cannot perceive or comprehend that God could provide for three of our children, but not for four. Rather, we maintain that our God, who can command the raven to supply for five of us, can also direct the birds to stuff the sixth's little mouth. We can step out in faith for three of our children, we can also do so for our fourth child.

Respectfully,

K. M. Wilhelm

I listened to the tape very intently while my world fell apart. I listened to Papa's plea to the Mission to include his fourth child in their support, but where was the plea for me, his fifth child? Did my parents not love me like the rest of my sisters and brothers? Did they not want me like they wanted their other children?

And why was that whole issue cloaked in secrecy all these years? Why was I told that I was too ill and weak to go to China with my family, instead of the truth?

I can still see Mutti sitting in our living room with us as we listened to the tape, unaware of its contents. Tears were streaming down her face as she realized my devastation. I begged Mutti for an answer, but she had none. She only said that Papa and my grandmother, without her consent, made the decision. I could not begin to imagine what she must have gone through, being a mother myself. How could my mother have been able to leave her little three-year-old child in the care of her husband's parents who were already elderly? How could she, how could my father? Answers would not come, and I felt so unwanted, unloved and cheated out of growing up with my own family, my parents, my brothers, my sisters.

The insecurity that I struggled with for so many years reared its ugly head and came to the foreground of my whole existence. I don't know how I would have survived without my husband during that time. He was my rock and my all; he loved me unconditionally, made me feel secure and was always there for me. Through depth of love and depth of grief my healing process began.

I found a deeper sense of forgiveness and love than I had ever known before and God, who is the healer of all wounds, was my constant companion and source of comfort. I discovered that I could learn even from the most adverse circumstances and experiences, and made peace with my life's past.

* * *

Our children continued to be a source of much joy to us, and we were so proud of each one of them.

The neighborhood in which we lived was not developing as we had hoped it would, and therefore we decided to find a house in another location. We were able to sell our current home and purchased a home on Skyline Drive in the north east part of Scottsbluff. We moved into our new house that was about five years old. It was in need of redecorating, but that was something we loved doing. Little by little the house became very comfortable and a home of which we were very proud of.

Steve was in Junior High School, and Donnie and Jenny were in Grade school, attending Longfellow School. The children walked to school, weather permitting, and often walked home from school as well.

When Donnie was about 10 years old, he told me one morning before he left for school that he needed to bring dress clothes for a certain occasion. Not questioning his motives too much, I packed his "Sunday best," and he happily went off to school. On his return home while he was walking, his dress pants slipped out of the bag that he was carrying, and he lost them. On Christmas Eve Donnie's present to us was a portrait of himself that was taken by Charlie Downey at Downey's Studio. It was taken the day he took his dress clothes to school and lost his dress pants on the way home. The picture was a wonderful surprise to us, and we were amazed that he was able to keep his studio visit a secret.

18

Schooley's Mountain, New Jersey

A short time after my father died, Ruth Bastam wrote to Mutti and said that she had promised Papa that she, Ruth, would take care of Mutti after his departure.

None of us had ever heard of this woman, who said she was connected with the Liebenzell Mission in Schooley's Mountain. She was German and worked as a nurse, but I don't know whether she was a registered nurse or not. She came to visit Mutti here in Scottsbluff several times and very clearly won a place in Mutti's heart. At the end, she almost split our family in half and caused, especially Bill and me, much grief. She made decisions for Mutti that should have been made by her family and totally took over her life. In 1968 she came to Scottsbluff one day with a trailer attached to her car and said that she was packing Mutti's things to take her to live in Schooley's Mountain. It came as quite a shock to us, and we were hurt that we had not been notified before hand. Mutti and Papa had always planned on living out their life in Schooley's Mountain, but we had hoped to have Mutti with us for a little while longer.

Ruth told Mutti said she was taking her away since we were not taking care of her properly. That was so untrue...

We had been noticing that Mutti was beginning to show signs of dementia and was often not thinking clearly. Her memory was failing her, especially her short-term memory. She remembered experiences from fifty years earlier, but could not recall what happened yesterday. Ruth packed up Mutti's personal belongings, stored other items at a friend's house, and rented the furnished house that we had so lovingly fixed up for my parents, to a Chinese friend by the name of Ruth Soong.

It was difficult to say good-bye to Mutti, but she was excited and anxious to be living in Schooley's Mountain. Another chapter was coming to a close...

* * *

A year later during a street construction project, the gas line of the house on Park View Lane was damaged, and the house blew up and was demolished. Bill and our sons were able to get into the burning house and rescued a few things, including the antique Chinese cabinet with the Pagoda, which was such a treasured family piece. The lot was later cleared of the debris and sold.

19

Business Opportunities

In the late 1960's, Bill sold his Tent and Awning Company, as well as his insulating business and became the manager of Lichter Duo Rest, which was a sister corporation of Magnolia Homes. Lichter Duo Rest was a factory that produced furniture and bedding for the Mobile Home Industry, as well as draperies for all the windows in their homes. He enjoyed working in that capacity, but soon yearned to have his own business again.

* * *

Our children enjoyed school and kept busy with their activities which Bill and I supported wholeheartedly. Jenny was taking piano lessons and also sang in the church junior choir. She had a sweet voice and had a solo when her choir presented the musical "Fishers of Men". She was nervous about it, but did very well.

When Jenny was about 11 years old, she fell off the bars in her grade school playground and had to have many stitches in her upper lip, inside and outside of her mouth. It happened during the last week of school before summer vacation.

Our doctor and good friend, Ron Nelson, did a beautiful job sewing and repairing Jenny's mouth with as few scars as possible remaining. We felt so sorry for her and wished we could have taken her pain away.

Steve and Don were both active in Boy Scouts and worked hard to achieve the highest rank they could. Attending the Boy Scout Camp at Laramie Peak, Wyoming was an always a summer highlight where both were inducted into the "Order of the Arrow." Steve achieved the rank of "Life" Scout and Don received his "Eagle Scout" award upon fulfilling all the requirements needed.

* * *

The local Community College approached me to teach conversational German again as I had done many years earlier. I agreed, and taught an evening class for many years. I enjoyed it immensely and made so many good friends.

Jenny and a group of her friends decided to join 4-H and I volunteered to be their leader. We had such a good time cooking, sewing, crafting and entering our products at the County Fair to be judged. I enjoyed working with the girls and was very proud of them and their accomplishments. Several of the girls won purple ribbons at the Fair, which is the highest honor given.

In 1972, Bill decided to go into business for himself again and start a drapery business of his own. We pondered long and hard over a name and came up with the name of: "Trim Line Draperies." The location was on East 16th Street, just east of the Post Office. Bill was able to obtain the account from Magnolia Homes and once again started making draperies for that company. He hired several seamstresses, bought the necessary sewing machines and other equipment and a new challenge was born. I started working part of the time to help out and to learn the business. Bill felt that it was the best insurance policy for me to know how to run the business in case something should happen to him.

Times often were not easy, and we worked hard and many nights to fill orders and to keep up with the demand of running a business. Steve and Don came to the store after school in the afternoon to do the cleaning; which was a big help to us, and they liked making a little extra allowance.

* * *

I had not seen my brothers in several years so we made the decision to take a trip to California and Oregon. Hans, Alice, Marty and Lita had moved back to San Jose from Brazil, and we were longing to see them again. Fred had married Yvonne Bowers in 1961, who we unfortunately had not met before. They had two children, Erich and Barbara, who we had only seen in pictures and we were most anxious to meet them all in person.

We packed up our station wagon, without air-conditioning, and headed west. It was a wonderful trip for all of us, and the kids had much fun with all the cousins. I felt good to have made the effort to see my brothers and their families and to mend some broken down communications.

While we were in Oregon, we went on a camping trip in the Portland area, with Fred and Yvonne and their two children. The adults were busy setting up the campsite and the children went exploring. The campground was set up with a series of pods; each held four camp-sides which all looked identical. There were walkways around the pods and through the trees that resembled tunnels and intrigued the children. It was very easy to get disoriented and somehow, Jenny got separated from her brothers and cousins, who found their way back to our campground, but Jenny became lost. Frantically we all took off in different directions searching for her, but to no avail. She had been missing for about forty-five minutes when Bill headed for the ranger station to report our missing little girl. When Bill arrived at the ranger station, Jenny spotted our car and saw her Dad. She came running and he caught her in his arms. It was a happy ending to a very frightening experience during the summer of 1972.

* * *

Steve was beginning his junior year in high school and was an excellent student. While he was still in junior high school he decided to go into the medical field and become a doctor. Our doctor friend, Ron Nelson, was his idol and he took him to his office at times to show him some medical procedures. Steve started working as an orderly at the hospital after he took a course at the college to qualify for that job. Working in a medical facility amplified his desire to become a doctor. He loved playing chess and was quite an accomplished player.

Steve played his violin in the orchestra and played for several high school musicals and concerts. The high school "A Cappella" choir as well as the church choir were other favorite extra curricular activities for Steve. Another past-time favorite for Steve was doing magic tricks. He enjoyed doing slight of hand and tricks with coins and cards and became quite an accomplished magician. I was never able to figure out how he did his tricks and that really frustrated my inquisitive mind, but Steve kept his secrets well hidden and didn't even share them with his own mother.

Don started taking piano lessons and showed a great talent for music. In his 5th grade in school he started learning the french horn, a difficult instrument, which he played very well.

* * *

On September 4, 1972, Bill's mother, Carrie Osborn, died of heart failure at the hospital in Scottsbluff. She was 76 years old and had been suffering from hardening of the arteries and congestive heart failure.

Mom, as I called her, was a wonderful mother-in-law to me and I loved her dearly. Her skills as a grandmother were exemplary and our children loved going to Grandma's house to be with her. She was generous, loving and kind, and left a big void in our family. Bill was very close to his mother and mourned her death deeply. Her funeral service was at the Methodist Church where she had been a very active member. Reverend Lloyd Bliss had a very comforting message and Gary Bacon sang some favorite family selections at the service. Jenny was especially close to her Grandma and when she stood at her casket crying, Aunt Clee, comforted her by saying that she would be her Grandma from then on. And she kept that promise. Aunt Clee was a sister of Bill's father and was very close to our family. She lived in Scottsbluff, and we often visited her at her home.

Bill's father, Art Osborn, had been married to his wife Carrie for almost 46 years.

He was lost after her death and felt very bereaved; life would be very different for him, without his Carrie at his side.

Arthur Elmer Osborn was born in 1901 in Broken Bow, Nebraska, to James Clement Osborn and Nancy Jane (Jennie) Gilkeson Osborn. Art was the only son among six sisters. In 1916, the family moved from Broken Bow, Nebraska to Scottsbluff, Nebraska, where Art, (Dad, as I called him), resided the rest of his life.

He was in business with his father, who was a building contractor. They were known as "Osborn and Son." Their business was flourishing in the 1920's and

1930's and their construction business built about 52 houses in Scottsbluff during that time alone. He later sold insulation and weather stripping for doors and windows. During the Second World War, he worked on defense projects in California, Utah and Wyoming until he opened The Scottsbluff Tent and Awning Company in 1945.

* * *

In the early 70's, I took several courses in " Interior Design" from the Design Institute in Chicago, Illinois, by correspondence. I loved it and did quite well, learning a lot and re-enforcing what I had learned in my Home-Economics classes while I was in school in Germany. The reason I wanted to educate myself further in the field of home decorating was to be able to apply it in our business. Bill felt the need to expand Trim Line and added a line of Custom Draperies to the Commercial Draperies that the company was manufacturing. I decided to become a full-time employee at Trim Line and thus Bill and I became a working team devoting our energy in different directions. Bill was handling the business affairs, as well as the commercial drapery accounts, while I was taking charge of the Custom Drapery sales and consulting with our clients on their selections of window treatments for their homes. I enjoyed my work immensely and found that I had a natural ability to work with the public. We were not spared our share of trials and tribulations of running a business and had our ups and downs, but Bill and I were determined to make a good business even better by perseverance, hard work and honesty. God was good to us and answered many prayers and for that we felt a deep sense of gratitude.

* * *

Steve and Don were teenagers by now and we treasured each day we had with them, knowing that soon they would leave home and be off to college. We had heard so many horror stories of teenage behavior and teenage problems and Bill and I asked ourselves often when that time would arrive. However, we had no complaints with our sons and by the grace of God that time never came. They were normal, active and busy guys who always showed us our due respect and love. For that we were so thankful.

When Steve and Don were old enough to carry guns, Bill took them pheasant hunting with him and taught them gun safety and responsibility for that sport. The boys loved going with their Dad, for it was an outing with just "guys," and they felt very grown-up. Their favorite part of the hunting day was stopping at the little diner in Hemingford in the middle of nowhere Nebraska, for lunch. They served the best cheeseburgers and french-fries in the area.

* * *

Our Methodist church had a very active youth ministry and a wonderful youth choir under the direction of Gary Bacon. Each summer they performed a Christian musical and took it on tours to perform in other churches. While Steve was in choir, the tour took them to Yellowstone Park, Spokane, Washington, and on to Seattle, Washington. It was a great experience for the young people and besides having a wonderful trip; they ministered to many congregations in other churches.

Steve often practiced his piano lesson while I was preparing dinner after coming home from work. I loved listening to him play and marveled at the discipline he demonstrated in many ways. He was inducted into the Scottsbluff High School Honor Society in his junior, as well as his senior year in High School and we were very proud of him for accomplishing this scholastic achievement. The choral music department was a real memory maker for Steve and he was involved in several musical productions, either playing the violin in the orchestra, or singing with the stage choir. Mr. Bacon was the Scottsbluff High School music director for many years and had a great impact on all of our children. While Steve was in his senior year in High School, entered the State Chess Tournament and won second place. What an accomplishment that was.

* * *

In 1973, Jenny got her first 10-speed bike and earned half of the money for it by cleaning at Trim Line and baby-sitting; it was a big purchase for her and she was thrilled with it. Later that year her greatest wish was fulfilled when her Dad got her a little puppy. It was a poodle and she named her "Gigi." She was Jenny's constant companion for many years to come.

* * *

After a very successful scholastic High School experience, our oldest son Steve graduated from Scottsbluff High School in the Spring of 1974 and was accepted to the University of Nebraska in Lincoln to start studying in the Fall of 1974. We took a trip to Lincoln to tour the campus of the University and to take

Steve for Freshman orientation. We were impressed with what we saw and heard, and felt confident to send our son to study at UNL.

It was an emotional day for me when Steve packed up his old station wagon and left for Lincoln. He was the first of our children to leave the nest of his parental comfort zone, but he was very excited to begin this new epoch in his life.

* * *

During the summer of 1974, we had alarming news from Schooley's Mountain of Mutti's failing health. I was able to fly to New Jersey to see my mother once more and it was a very rewarding experience for me. Her eyes were beginning to get dimmer and dimmer and death was imminent. She was mostly living in the past and must have remembered me as a little girl, not as an adult. When she saw me she said: "Oh, you have grown up." Her smile was still ever-present and she did not complain.

Once again, I was so sad that I had missed so many years of being her daughter and being able to claim her as my mother.

My dear, sweet Mutti died on August 24, 1974, at the age of 78 years. The family was very grateful that Eva was at her side when she went on to Glory. How happy she must have been to be reunited with Papa and her beloved daughter Esther.

The following is what my brother Hans wrote upon hearing of our Mother's death.

IN HIS PRESENCE

"Seventy years are given us! And some may even live to eighty. But even the best of these years are often emptiness and pain: soon they disappear, and we are gone..." Ps. 90:10

This verse flashed into my mind when I received the word of my mother's passing on August 24, in Schooley's Mountain, New Jersey. How good God has been to us! For forty-three years she has been my mother, and a good mother, too. Raising a family in primitive China was not always easy. Yet, she never complained, but used her resourcefulness to make our childhood days, happy indeed. My mother's life has been full, beginning with her years of service as deaconess of the "Friedenshort," the home for motherless children, 26 years as a missionary in China and her years as a pastor's wife in America.

And yet, all these years have only produced a growing sweetness and gentleness of character that made her a saint indeed. Were her 78 years only "emptiness and pain"? Certainly not! She had learned to be satisfied from her earliest youth with His loving kindness, which gave her constant joy to the end of her life. Now she has finished her course, she has received her crown, she can rest from her labor, and she is in His presence!

Mutti was buried in Schooley's Mountain next to her beloved husband.

Standing at her grave, a fierce realization came upon me that Mutti's passing signified the end of an era, and we, her children, inherited the awesome responsibility of a new generation.

* * *

Don's interest in sports led him to football and track. He was intimidated by the athletic boys who were bigger than he was, but he was quick and made the track team, running the 880 and the two-mile. He also made the 9th grade football team and was so proud to wear his team's jersey to school on game days.

Don played French horn in Mrs. Diers' band and earned first chair in the horn section. Mrs. Diers ran a pretty tight ship and directed an exceptionally professional sounding band. The kids had to be very disciplined to play in the band, but it paid off in the long run. Later, Don played in the marching and concert band in high school, reclaiming his first chair in the horn section.

In the fall of 1974, while playing football, Don injured his knee, curtailing many of his activities. He was in the 9th grade, a freshman in High School.

During this time Don discovered girls and had crushes on many girls, Liz, Leanne, Merry and others.

Church activities were high on the list for Don and his best friend, Bill Bliss: Youth fellowship, choir, bible studies and prayer breakfasts. Often the girls who were active in the same activities were the incentive for the strong interest. Oh, the mystery of puberty...

Don was chosen to play a part in many high school musical productions. In his first musical, while in the sixth grade, Don had the leading role in the High School production of "Amahl and the Night Visitors." We were very excited to watch him on stage. Next came "The Music Man." He was so excited to wear the 50-year-old band uniforms the Scottsbluff High School acquired. Don performed in several musical productions while he was in high school and during his senior year had the lead in "Show Boat". He did a super job and we went to see it several times. Steve made a special trip from Lincoln to watch his brother perform and sing.

Don was very outgoing and loved going to dances and parties and was the "mood-setter" in our home. I remember teaching him how to dance in our living room several nights before a special dance to which he was invited. He wore brown and beige striped "dress" bell -bottom pants to the dance and felt pretty groovy.

Don was a good student and Mom and Dad made sure that there was sufficient time for studies during school days.

* * *

Jenny was in Junior High School by now and was very busy with her activities. She loved being in Job's Daughters, learned to play the flute and played in the school band, was active in the youth group in church, sang in the choir and played hand-bells. Besides being busy with all of her activities, she made plenty of time for her many friends, with the telephone as the great tool for communication.

Her favorite recreation after school was jumping on the trampoline and it paid off. She was the only student in her P.E. class to receive an A for her efforts.

I remember the first boy friend she had. His name was David and he bought her a ring at Woolworth, which cost one dollar.

20

Return to my Roots

In early 1975, Bill and I decided we would take a trip to Germany that summer. It was a "wish come true" for me. I had dreamed of going back to Germany, my old home, for many years, and now it would become a reality.

For so long I had desired to show my husband where I grew up and introduce him to the many relatives and friends who were living in Germany.

For six months we waited to get a special visa to enter East Germany; the special permission arrived just in time before we were to leave on our long-awaited journey.

We departed Stapleton airport in Denver on June 8, 1975, on a Jumbo Jet 474 for Toronto, Canada for refueling; from Toronto we flew to Berlin, Germany. My excitement was indescribable and I could not believe that I would soon set foot on German ground again. 25 years ago, almost to the date, I had left East Germany to begin my incredible journey to America.

At the most famous crossing point, "Checkpoint Charlie," we crossed the border from West to East Berlin. We were glad when the ordeal was completed and were able to leave the station at the border. From a distance I could see my Aunt Marthel and cousin Wolfgang Richter waiting for us; what a joy it was to see them again. Another cousin, who lived in Berlin, joined us and after we had a meal together, we left Berlin by car to travel to Zschorlau, my little hometown. When we arrived, our first stop was at the Police Station where we had to sign in. When we left one week later, we had to check out at the Police Station.

Bill and I were overwhelmed by the warm and loving welcome we received from my many relatives; and although Bill did not speak the German language he was able to communicate with them quite well. The eyes and gestures spoke volumes of the love they held for us in their hearts. We had a wonderful time, visiting, touring the area, eating and drinking their special wines and cognacs and sharing photos from years gone by.

We were bombarded with many questions about our country, the "Free World." Questions like: "Do you really have machines to dry your clothes and wash your dishes? Do most Americans belong to cults? Why do you have so many poor people in soup lines?" Another cousin asked me: "Is it really true that you can travel from one state to another state in America without permission?"

My Aunt Marthel and her husband were our hosts while we visited in Zschorlau. They lived in an apartment house that was a fairly new structure, built by the communist government, but it did not have any modern conveniences. They moved into their apartment three years earlier and were still without a telephone...

Each time we left the apartment building, we had to sign a registry and when we returned we were obligated to sign the registry again. We were able to travel from one village, or town, to another during the day, but had to return to the apartment house by night, every night. It was pretty obvious that we were monitored at all times. This made us feel quite uncomfortable, almost frightened, knowing it was common knowledge in my hometown that I had left the country illegally.

Walking through the little towns it broke my heart to see my beautiful "Erzgebirg" in such utter distress. Houses were literally falling apart. Building material and paint was almost non-existent, leaving towns and villages in unbelievable disrepair. Oh, how I ached for my dear relatives...

Christians paid a high price for following the Lord, but were so rich in refined faith and character as a result. We were deeply touched by the spirit of gratefulness and generosity of my loved ones. They possessed so little, but shared all they had with us, so lovingly.

Their sparkling sense of humor under such a harsh system, and their commitment to each other, was remarkable.

After almost two weeks of being with relatives we boarded the "Interzonen Zug," (inter-zonal train) which took us back to West Germany. While we were in Zschorlau, we had been told to record any items that we purchased, or that were given to us, and to present to the border police on the train; every item had to be accounted for. We carefully listed every item, no matter how small and insignificant it might have seemed to us. However, we forgot to list a small polished rock that was a souvenir my cousin purchased for me when we visited an old mine. This oversight almost caused us serious problems.

In the middle of the night, our train came to a sudden stop at the border and every passenger was checked and rechecked, bodily, as well as all of their luggage and bags. The policewoman who was in charge of our compartment on the train found the small rock but could not find it on our list of purchases. I explained to her in German that I had simply forgotten to write it down and her reply was "what else have you forgotten to write down?" and the search was on. She searched throughout our luggage and bags for a long time while we held our breath; she found nothing else and we were released from her clutches. We were fortunate, many other people were not.

Finally, after two hours, the train's wheels started to roll again and when we left East Germany, crossing the border. Seeing the metal fence running the entire length of the country, with automatic firing devices to shoot anyone who tried to leave, brought tears of gratitude and joy for the freedom we take so for granted.

Bill and I were extremely happy and relieved when we were back in West Germany on safe ground.

The next stop on our trip was in Koeln, where we visited my cousin and wife before we flew to Paris. My sister Eva and her family were living in France during that time and we were most anxious to spend some time with them.

Eva's husband, Johannes, met us at the airport in Paris and took us to their home in LaCelle St. Clue where the family awaited our arrival. We met Eva and Johannes's children and had a most wonderful time with my sister's family.

They showed us Paris and touring that famous city was most enjoyable and very special. We saw all the well-known places in Paris, such as Place DeLa Concorde, the Church of the Sacre-Coeur, the Eiffel Tower, the Notre Dam as well as the beautiful Palace of Versailles. We were so impressed with all we saw and loved every day of our trip. After a most delightful time in Paris, Bill and I took a train to Strasburg. It was an unforgettable train ride taking us through beautiful country. After visiting more cousins in southern Germany, Eva and Johannes joined us and we traveled together to Switzerland and other areas in Germany.

The Eiger, Moench and Jungfrau mountains and the picturesque, unique little town of Grindlewald will forever stay in our memory.

After a month long trip to Germany, France and Switzerland we flew back to the United States and arrived in Denver on July 9th, 1975. Our children awaited us at the Airport and we were very happy to see each other. We had so much to tell them and were eager to hear how they had fared without us.

To be back on American soil was an absolute joy to us and we felt so privileged and proud to live in a country where freedom is available to all. Freedom is what America is all about...

Epilog

And the Walls Come Tumbling Down!

October 4, 1990

"German dream comes true! The two Germanys ended 45 years of division with a blaze of fireworks and the pealing of church bells, declaring the creation of a new German nation in the heart of Europe. Germany is re-united! A miracle has happened and a nation has been set free."

I was riveted to the television set far into the night watching this incredible piece of history develop. I never thought that I would experience this historic event in my lifetime. To see the borders open up and the wall come down right in front of my eyes, was absolutely unbelievable to me. I was so happy for our family in East Germany, who had longed for this freedom ever since World War II.

The opening of the borders brought about a family reunion at my sister Eva's home in Ludwigshafen, Germany, with many of the relatives traveling to the West for the very first time since the Wall was erected. It was an indescribable joy for all of us to be re-united again. Two years later, in 1992, another family gathering was held in Scottsbluff at our home. The world became smaller and traveling became a dream come true for many of my relatives, who were able to fly across the ocean in an airplane, a new experience for all of them.

God has been so good to us, and we are so grateful for all of our blessings.

The years between 1975 and the present have been filled with an abundance of joys, and sorrows, but have been rewarding and rich in experiences. We have lost many of our loved ones, among them Bill's father, our Aunt Clee, Bill's sister Donna and many others. We have also mourned the death of a number of our friends.

Bill and I have traveled extensively, and have seen many places in Europe, Jamaica, and Hawaii, as well as incredibly beautiful areas in our own country, the United States of America.

Our children have brought us much joy and pride with their accomplishments and we are so grateful to God for their continued support and love for us.

Steve fulfilled his dream of becoming a doctor and is practicing medicine in Omaha, Nebraska. His chosen specialty is Family Practice. After graduating from medical school in Omaha, Nebraska, Steve married

Barbara Nissen in Omaha where they are raising their three children, Anneliese, Becky and Neil. They are such a joy to us. Barb was a wonderful addition to our family and we are so fortunate to have her as a daughter-in-law. A nurse by profession, Barb chose to be a stay-at-home Mom and has made a wonderful home for her family. She is very creative and a very talented seamstress as well as a "Master Gardener." Our visits to Omaha are always a special treat and we love spending time with the Osborn family as often as possible.

* * *

Don graduated from the University of Colorado with a degree in music and has pursued his passion for music throughout the years. Don's background in music includes a broad range of creative and administrative positions. Currently he is a music business consultant, writing music business and marketing plans and is living in Vancouver, British Columbia. His son Tyler, who lives in Vancouver, is an outstanding athlete and is Don's pride and joy. He is a very solid and bright young man and we cherish the time we get to spend with him. It is such a thrill for us to watch Tyler play football and we love attending his games whenever possible, though we regret that we live so far apart. Don was divorced from Tyler's mother when Tyler was two years old.

Jenny graduated from Cottey College in Nevada, Missouri and Park's Business School in Denver, Colorado. After completing her education, she was employed at a large manufacturing firm in Denver where she worked in the accounting department of the firm. While working and living in Denver she met Pat Bashford, who stole her heart. Pat grew up with a family of ten siblings and is a very compassionate, patient and kind man; so perfect for Jenny. In 1985, Jenny and Pat were married in our Methodist Church in Scottsbluff. They have three wonderful children, Sarah, Andy and David. Pat is an Electrical Engineer and graduated from the University of Colorado in Boulder. He currently designs computer chips for a company in Fort Collins where he and his family reside. Jenny has had a very fulfilling vocation as a stay-at-home Mom and is a very devoted wife and mother. Besides making a lovely home for her family, Jenny is very involved in her children's activities, volunteering at school and church. Some of her favorite hobbies include scrap booking, traveling, cooking, and entertaining friends.

* * *

We adore our seven grandchildren and they have been a source of great joy to Bill and me. We consider ourselves very fortunate and feel so blessed with their talents, bright minds and loving natures.

* * *

In 1995, after serving the valley for almost 30 years in the Drapery and Decorating Business, Bill and I decided to sell our business and join the throngs of retired citizens. We have enjoyed our life of leisure and are grateful for the time we are able to spend with family and friends, traveling and focusing on hobbies and staying healthy.

* * *

My sister Peggie and her husband Jerry Ross, as well as my brother Fred and his wife Yvonne moved back to Scottsbluff a number of years ago, and we are happy to have family in close proximity. My brother Hans and his wife Alice, live in California and my sister Eva, and her husband Johannes, are living in Germany. We are all staying in close contact with each other and I am grateful that one of my father's predictions that he made in 1935 did NOT come true. I have a close and loving relationship with all of my siblings and for that I am truly thankful.

I recently read some old letters that were written by Papa to his sister in Germany, soon after they returned to China.

He said and I quote:

> *We are longing to receive news from home, and are eager to know how our little child is faring. We miss our little sweet Anita very much, and have decided that, if we had to do it over again, we would not leave her behind. It is very hard for us, because we realize that Anita will never have a true and close relationship and contact with her parents and her siblings. We brought this sacrifice for Jesus and we pray, that He will bless our little daughter in abundance.*

The words in this letter were a tremendous gift to me and filled my heart with gratitude. Knowing that my parents had regrets for leaving me behind, and saw this action as a sacrifice, is very comforting to me. Their sacrifice resulted in the fruition of a full, rewarding life, surrounded by a loving family, caring friends, and the privilege of living in a free country.

ISBN 141201578-2

9 781412 015783